"Like the Irish writer Brian Moore who Weber constructs a spare, carefully plo thriller....Resonates long after the book is closed."
— *Houston Chronicle*

"Taut, quick, and original: a good mix of real suspense with an intelligent story."
— *Kirkus Reviews*

"A beautifully crafted, tightly controlled story, with wonderfully sensual descriptions of art and landscape... Highly recommended."
— *Library Journal* (starred review)

"[An] emotionally involving thriller that is propelled by psychological intensity...Weber remains a writer to be cherished, with the added, and quite rare, virtue of never writing a word too much."
— *Publishers Weekly* (starred review)

"Tightly wrought, atmospheric thriller...Weber's descriptive powers—whether depicting the elusive layers of character or the rocky, cloud-wrapped Irish countryside—are precise and evocative."
— *Atlanta Journal-Constitution*

"[A] gem of a book."
— *Norfolk Virginian-Pilot*

"Through her tautly orchestrated and increasingly frightening plot, Weber ponders a number of complex issues which she counterpoints one against the other with real finesse....*The Music Lesson* is a finely wrought and controlled piece of writing that explores the nature and danger of obsession. Sensual, closely observed, the prose captures the smell and physicality of rural Ireland, seducing the reader into the tangible world of this particular fictitious construct."
— *The London Observer*

"Beautifully wrought, accomplished, and engaging."
— *The Irish Independent*

The MUSIC LESSON

Katharine Weber

PICADOR USA
NEW YORK

For information on Picador USA Reading Group Guides, as well as ordering, please contact the Trade Marketing department at St. Martin's Press.
Phone: 1-800-221-7945 extension 763
Fax: 212-677-7456
E-mail: trademarketing@stmartins.com

Library of Congress Cataloging-in-Publication Data

Weber, Katharine.
  The music lesson / Katharine Weber.
    p. cm.
  ISBN 0-312-25285-4
  1. Vermeer, Johannes, 1632–1675—Appreciation—Fiction. 2. Women art historians—United States—Fiction. 3. Irish Republican Army—Fiction. 4. Art thefts—Fiction. I. Title.
  PS3575.E2194 M87 2000
  813'.54—dc21
                                                    99-54978
                                                         CIP

First published in the United States by Crown Publishers, Inc.

10 9 8 7 6 5 4 3 2

For my mother, who loves words

———

A Note to the Reader

———

In a novel, the fictions are not necessarily limited to character and plot. The world has never seen this particular painting by Vermeer, because it does not quite exist. The Vermeer at Buckingham Palace is a different painting altogether, and I have no reason to believe that it has ever been the object of a ransom plot. While there was a recent Vermeer exhibition at the Mauritshuis in The Hague, it did not actually take place in the month of January. It would be very rude to write about my neighbors, so I haven't. There is no village of Ballyroe in West Cork, but if there were, it might be near the village of Ardfield. I have no knowledge of any IRA splinter group calling itself the Irish Republican Liberation Organization.

K. W.

It pained him that he did not know well what politics meant and that he did not know where the universe ended.

JAMES JOYCE, *A Portrait of the Artist as a Young Man*

The
MUSIC
LESSON

———

19th of January, raining

———

S HE'S BEAUTIFUL. Surely, there is nothing more interesting to look at in all the world, nothing, than the human face. Her gaze catches me, pins me down, pulls me in.

It's dark and cold and wet. Why am I here and what am I doing? The entire muddy countryside—cows, sheep, pigs included—seems to be gripped by a seasonal despair in these short days. The shrill, thrilling wind blows into my bones and stays there. There are moments when I wonder if I will ever be warm again.

I look at my face in the mirror and it seems far away, indistinct, less real than hers.

Katharine Weber

◻

I'm just back from a four-mile walk in the blowing rain to O'Mahoney's, the nearest shop, where I bought some groceries and a newspaper, and this accounting ledger (the only notebook on his shelf), and had my first conversation of the day, with Mr. O'Mahoney, as follows, in its entirety:

"With that fuchsia hedge all overgrown at the junction because the county council didn't trim it yet, though I couldn't say why that is at all, they should have trimmed it in September, but the council cut more corners than hedges in this village, that eejit flyin' down the road in the bread van almost took the nose off ye, miss. Better mind that road—ye were very nearly a black spot just now. I was watchin' out the window, just havin' a peep to see if there was any chance of the rain liftin' a bit. Which there isn't. Aren't ye afraid out there all by yer lonesome in the cottage with just old Denny's ghost to talk to? Thinkin' of leavin' us in another few days' time, I'd say? Ye've stuck it out a fortnight, isn't that right? Willy, the postman, was sayin' yesterday. He had a letter for ye from the States. Did ye get that all right? He was on his way to ye when we met at the church cross, and when I saw him later, he said ye weren't at home at all and he'd left the post on a chair. I think he said on a chair, but more likely it wasn't a chair at all, but a stool, the creepie by the door Denis used to sit on to pull off his

2

wellies. Had enough of yer own company, then? January is no time a'tall for tourists. No time at all. Come back in May. Now that's the season for ye. Ye come back when the air is soft. That's the thing. On a Sunday after Mass when the air is soft and ye go out for a bit of a spin—my sister and myself, we like to take a bit of a rug to spread against the damp and she makes the sangwitches and we have our tea in the sun in my cousin John's field on the cliff out your way when the grass is sweet and clovery—that can be mighty altogether."

"I'm just fine, thanks, Mr. O'Mahoney. Do you have any more of that Wexford cheddar?"

"No, no, no, not a bit, not a bit—yer little lump was left from Christmas and I was happy enough to sell the last of it to ye, and I won't be havin' it again until the summer months. The locals don't have any truck with fancy grub, like. The tourist season's when ye'll be findin' the high-class sorts of bits and pieces a person like yerself would want to be havin'. The tourist season, like. Which this is not, in case ye haven't noticed."

I have yet to decide if Kieran O'Mahoney with his downturned smile that isn't a smile is even specifically interested in me, or slightly hostile to American tourists, or if his inquisitive stream of chatter is just his usual line of talk on a gray January day. I also have yet to decide exactly when he draws breath.

The only other shop in Ballyroe is across the street,

farther down, at the bottom of the village. It's even more sparsely stocked, with little more than single rows of dusty tins of beans, obscure brands of cleaning products, dog-eared Maeve Binchy paperbacks, and last summer's flypaper.

I am loyal to O'Mahoney's. As if it mattered, as if I have lived here all my life and plan to go on living here for the rest of my life, I have a preference. I don't frequent the other shop, Dunne's. I don't give them my custom.

The proprietress there is a snoopy woman, Annie Dunne, who has half of Kieran O'Mahoney's charm and twice his energy for sly, presumptive interrogatives. She's somewhere between forty and sixty is my best guess. I suppose she's pleasant-looking from a distance, in an ordinary pale Irish sort of way. But, up close, her eyes are cold, her skin has the secret age and fine wrinkles of an elderly nun, and the set of her lips is cruel. Annie Dunne gives me the creeps.

She sits in the window by the till on a high stool so she can keep an eye on the whole village. I'm sure she monitors my visits to O'Mahoney's. Unfortunately, she's a skilled baker of scones, a basket of which is usually sitting on her counter beside a stack of sticky little wooden frames of comb honey from her own bees.

Tempted thus on very wet days when I have been reluctant to turn around immediately and start the walk back to the cottage, I have stopped into Dunne's on three separate occasions, telling myself each time that I'm not really giving her my business, that I'm just buying some scones. And the one time, some honey. Though after my first encounter with Annie, I meant for it to be my last. She affects friendliness, but there's something really sinister about her; she might not mind baking me some special thumbtack scones just for the hell of it.

Not that I would give Kieran O'Mahoney the satisfaction of agreeing, I have indeed noticed that I seem to be the only tourist, so-called. There are few people at large of any description. Ballyroe has only about sixty year-round inhabitants, hardly any children (which suits me), and today, as on most days, I never met a car the entire two-mile walk back along the undulating lane out to Gortbreac Cove, above which the cottage is perched. In the drumming rain, with the thin straps of the carrier bag cutting through my soaked gloves into my numb fingers, I tried to figure how it could possibly be that each route, both into the village and out again, seems predominantly uphill.

The pockets of the "waterproof" I bought last week from Mr. O'Mahoney—it had lain in a filmy plastic sack on a low shelf in the back of the shop with a strange assortment of goods (a tub of stove black, a giant sheep thermometer, and extraterrestrial-looking bits of hardware for milking machines) for such a long time that its price was marked in shillings and he let me have it for four pounds—filled with water before I had gone halfway. When I got to the cottage, I undressed and dropped my sodden clothes just inside the door, in the mudroom.

I believe that walking in a windy Irish downpour wearing a porous mackintosh over an Irish sweater over a flannel shirt and blue jeans is to be wetter than when you stand naked in a shower. Now I'm in a change of clothes with a pot of tea and some chocolate digestive biscuits in front of the fire, drying my boots (and a wadded ten-pound note from my jeans pocket) on the warm hearth slates at my feet.

These are not complaints. I am happy here. At forty-one, I have never had fewer creature comforts and yet I have not been this content in a long time. This rough alien place feels like home. I have come here with a passionate commitment. For the first time in years, I wake up each day with a purpose. And, of course, I am not alone. I am never alone, whatever the village may think. Because she is here. And that is why I am here.

Everything I have ever thought I knew about the rest of my life has shifted in the last two months.

I've just lived through some agonizingly suspenseful days. How, in such a short space of time, have I come to alter my life so radically and in so many ways?

She's here. I can hardly believe it after all the waiting. There's nothing for me to do now but wait for further word from Mickey. So I'm at a standstill for the moment, in a timeless, motionless vacuum like the eye of a hurricane when the sun comes out for a brief moment. Of course, it's not yet safe to go out, because the other half of the storm is coming. What have I done?

This account is not meant for anyone's eyes. No, I don't suppose I could really mean that. Of course I imagine these words being read someday. But when I say it isn't meant for anyone's eyes, I don't mean it in the sense of one of those novel manuscripts people keep in a drawer, insisting they don't care if anyone else ever reads it or not.

The people I have known who do that, I am convinced, have no faith in themselves as writers and know, deep down, that the novel is flawed, that they don't know how to tell the story, or they don't understand what the story is, or they haven't really got a story to tell. The manuscript in the drawer *is* the story.

My *story* is the story, not writerly ambitions. Because I don't think of myself as a writer at all; I am free of anxiety that the words I choose must be the very best words. My mind is far more attuned to the visual world; I'm an art historian who has a basic skill at writing, at the art of describing artlessly. That's all.

My motive is primarily that of an art historian

reporting on events, cataloging a sequence of facts, making a scholar's record. Though I know, logically, it's impossible to attempt objectivity—I'm *inside* this—I am nevertheless compelled, by my training and by my nature, to try. Is it grandiose of me to imagine that it's important that my observations, my *explanation*, should exist in the world?

It is not my intention for this notebook to come to light in my lifetime. It is possible that the day may come when I myself feel that it is necessary to destroy these pages—and that day may be as soon as next week. But if it seems reasonable for this account to survive me, by the time these words are ever read by those who might be interested, it will be when the events described herein will have played out to the end, one way or another.

My name is Patricia Dolan. It's an Irish name, something people here keep pointing out to me, as if my being an American means that I might not have a clue that my forebears were ever from anywhere else and my presence here is entirely random coincidence. It's the part I play, albeit with reluctance. The amiable American tourist possessing neither curiosity nor a sense of history. There's an Irish fascination with the quotidian American lack of consciousness of history and context. I mean the way most Americans have a cultural amnesia for personal family history.

The United States is a conceited nation with shallow roots, and what happened before living memory doesn't seem to interest most people I know at home. We like living in our new houses with our new furniture, on our new streets in new neighborhoods. Everything is disposable and everything is replaceable. Personal family history can feel simply irrelevant in our new world, beyond the simplest national identifications, and even those can get sort of vague for people. I remember a boy in high school who told the history teacher that he was "half Italian, half Polish, half English, half German, and one-quarter Swedish." I think one of the reasons so many of us are disconnected from our histories is because none of it happened where we live in the present; the past, for so many, is a faraway place across an ocean.

So what do the people here in the village make of me? Not much, I hope. I imagine that most of the Ballyroe locals have encountered numerous American tourists in possession of an Irish name that they can't pronounce correctly and who don't even know with certainty from what county in Ireland their ancestors fled just two or three generations back. Tourists like that don't begin to understand the way history is still playing out today in the six counties in the North.

They don't bother to comprehend how it's been these past few hundred years, or, more to the point, these last couple of decades. They come to Ireland to have fun in the pubs and see the beautiful landscape and buy a nice sweater and carry home a souvenir shillelagh and some Waterford crystal, and they don't know what's going on. That's all the Ballyroe natives expect of me.

But I do know what's going on. There's an irony at work here. I'm in Ireland for the first time, right at the heart of my Dolan and O'Driscoll origins, and instead of throwing open my arms to embrace my own—possibly every other farmer in this village—I have to keep to myself and stay hidden, camouflaged as an ordinary tourist.

It feels now as if my whole life has been a preparation for what I am doing. But I must keep the lowest of profiles. I have managed to do this in part by the simple act of staying out of the village pubs. Since I don't go to Mass, either, I'm left out of village life.

Too much conversation is the last thing I would need, and I'm not a drinker anyway. A woman alone here is likely to be speculated about no matter what, according to Mickey, so I shouldn't give anyone anything to ponder. It doesn't take much for the imaginative Irish to start thinking up stories to go with people and their circumstances.

Anyway, I have no desire to venture into any of the three pubs in the village. They're all so dark-looking, and they aren't exactly inviting to an outsider, with curtains muffling the windows as if for an imminent air-raid exercise.

I am in awe of the perpetual tumult of the sea. I am moved by the still place on the horizon where the sky begins. I am stirred by the soaring and dipping fields that make the landscape into a rumpled green counterpane. I thought I would never have such powerful feelings again. I thought I would live through the rest of my life having experiences, and thoughts, but I never thought I would again feel deeply—I was convinced that my wounds had healed and become thick scars, essentially numb.

In a way, she's incongruous here. But the contrast of her elegance with these simple surroundings isn't really jarring, because tranquillity and timelessness transcend everything else.

20th of January, still raining

———

THE FIRST TIME I heard Mickey's voice on the telephone, it was midafternoon on November the twelfth, the day after Veteran's Day. I thought it was somebody calling to tell me something had happened to Pete. When your father is a policeman, even a crotchety retired one, you always worry that someday you'll pick up the phone and it's going to be a strange voice with the news you never want to hear. I was in the slide room of the Frick Art Reference Library where I work, sorting through an unexpectedly jumbled Fragonard drawer, when the call was put through to me from the reference desk where I usually sit.

"Is this Patricia Dolan?"

"Speaking."

"The Patricia Dolan who is the daughter of Peter Dolan?"

"Yes—is something wrong with Pete? Is he all right? Has something happened?"

"No, not at all, not at all." This was when I noticed the Irish accent. "This is yer cousin, then, Patricia Dolan. Michael O'Driscoll is my name, and we're cousins."

"Where are you calling from, Michael?" Relieved now, I was curious. He sounded young. I envisioned a student with a knapsack, run away from university, seeking his fortune in America.

"The call box in the park, just across Fifth Avenue from yer very grand Frick Collection," he said. "I was hopin' you could come away out of there and we could have a cup of tea and a chat. I haven't got the price of admission, and anyway, I don't know how to find you in with the books."

He *was* young—sixteen years younger than I—with a deceptive baby face. Piercing blue eyes, like Pete's, not mine—I've got my mother's topaz brown eyes—met my gaze each time I turned to glance at him as we walked the few blocks up Madison Avenue to eat at E.A.T. (It's a casual but outrageously expensive restaurant, so I figured I would treat. I have an irrational love of the place, an addictive relationship to the bread sticks, and I cherish any opportunity to glimpse a certain famous writer with a long white braid who lives in the neighborhood, occupying a corner table, furtively supplementing her meal with take-out soup from the coffee shop across the street.)

Michael O'Driscoll didn't have the traditional "map of Ireland" kind of features and coloring, yet there was something subtly Irish about his face. An amused wariness. Our hair was almost the same color—a beigy no color. He needed a haircut. We were about the same height, which is to say I'm slightly tall for a woman and he's slightly short for a man. In a passing shop window, I noted the symmetry of our matching reflections. We could have been brother and sister.

When he smiled, which he did frequently, his eyes crinkled and he looked a decade older than he did in the brief moments when his face was between expressions and he looked like anybody and nobody.

His clothes weren't exactly shabby, but his corduroys and flannel shirt and sweater, while clean, showed signs of wear. He had an easy, surefooted stride, a grace, really, yet he was very watchful, somehow very careful, taking everything in as we walked.

He occupied the space beside me in a way that suddenly reminded me of someone I knew and had had a slight crush on years ago, Rick something, an Outward Bound guide from Seattle whom I met a few times when a college friend who had gone out with him was showing him around New York. Now there was a man who seemed capable of anything at all. Rick Green. He had such alertness and interest in his surroundings, and this same appraising wariness.

Rick clearly regarded the streets of New York as, quite literally, a concrete jungle, and he had to be talked out of a caving expedition to explore a disused portion of the BMT subway line. Sometimes I meet men who remind me of Rick and I picture him again for a moment, tackling the wilderness of New York with his earnest West Coast skills, rappelling down the Seagram Building, weaving a hammock under the trees in Central Park out of a spool of dental floss, cooking a meal over a flaming copy of the *Daily News*. I do love competence in a man.

On the way to the restaurant, Michael O'Driscoll told me to call him Mickey, and by the second corner we had sorted through the O'Driscolls and figured how it was that we were related. Strangely enough, right up to that moment, it had never occurred to me in any real way that I had contemporary relations in Ireland. Which is really odd, now that I think about it, given all the passion about Irish politics in my family. It might have had something to do with my grandfather Paddy's being so cut off from his parents only a short couple of generations out of Ireland.

Between my father and my grandfather, what I knew of my Irish family history seemed all in the past. My thoughts about Ireland in the present had been, right up to this moment, entirely mythic, entirely political. And theoretical. In light of where I sit as I write these words, it's almost impossible to believe, but that's how it was. My Irish relations existed as daguerreotypes in my head. Mickey's sudden appearance was almost shocking, like something from a movie, as if an ancestor had risen from the grave and come to call and now we were walking up Madison Avenue together, having a chat.

Mickey told me that he had grown up in the village of Rosscarbery, in County Cork, before leaving to attend Trinity College in Dublin—the first family member to do so, he said with pride—and he seemed pleased that my automatic response was to identify Rosscarbery as the birthplace of O'Donovan Rossa and Michael Collins.

"You've been home, of course?"

"Never."

"A sin you'll soon have to rectify," Mickey said merrily as he held the door to E.A.T. open for me. Two girls of about twelve in Nightingale-Bamford uniforms ducked under his arm as if they owned the world, and Mickey caught my eye and we grinned at each other over their heads before we went inside.

That sort of moment is rarely easy for me. Katie

would be eight now. Would she be reading the *Little House* books? Rollerblading? Agitating for pierced ears? She had just started piano lessons.

Mickey said something as we waited to order about how glad he was to have been able to find me. I said something about how I was glad, too, while privately noting an almost giddy feeling of overwhelming relief at his presence, as if I had been expecting him for a long time—the way, at La Guardia, when I'm waiting for Pete to come in on the shuttle, I keep scanning the faces of strangers until finally one of the strangers turns into Pete.

At that moment sitting with Mickey, waiting for our food, I felt something I hadn't felt for a long time—it was a sense of not being alone. No, it was more than that. I felt safe.

It didn't occur to me to question how he had managed to locate me at work—on reflection, the more likely thing would have been a call to Pete or a message on my machine, since Pete's listed in Boston and I'm in the Manhattan phone book.

I've since learned that information is one of Mickey's specialties. And, of course, I know now that Mickey was not looking for Pete; he was looking for me.

Over soup and bread—some days I don't feel up to the lofty conversation at the elaborate and formal staff lunch at the Frick, and this had been one of those days, so I'd had a yogurt at my desk, with a few pages of an Iris Murdoch novel, *The Sea, the Sea*—"One of the secrets of a happy life is continuous small treats" being an important nugget of wisdom therefrom—Mickey told me that he was on his first visit to America and he was feeling like an idiotic "toorist." He was here for six weeks, he said, having come because there was a slim chance at landing an apprenticeship doing fine cabinetry with an Irish guy he knew who had emigrated from Kilkenny and now operated a hugely successful workshop in SoHo. (I had, in fact, recently seen an article about the workshop in the Sunday *New York Times*.)

He said he was staying in a flat in Rego Park, Queens, which belonged to a school friend of his who worked for Aer Lingus. When I smiled at that—at all of it, not just the "flat" but also the grand tone he lent to "Rego Park" and "Queens"—Mickey touched my wrist and laughed and corrected himself, calling it an "apartment" with a ridiculous fake American twang. By pastries and coffee, I had fallen in love. I think it took Mickey a little longer than that.

Of course, he knew all about me. He knew, for instance, that I had never traveled to Ireland. He knew everything. I suppose I should be furious that over the next days and weeks he let me tell him in my own way in my own time about my growing up, my motherless child-hood, all about Paddy and Pete, and then my college years, my work, Sam, Katie, the accident, and about the one brief and not terribly successful relationship I had had (pathetically, with a married visiting lecturer in art history at Columbia, who came to see me about some slides) in the empty time from then to now, all of which he knew.

I suppose, too, that I should have been more suspicious of Mickey's vague plans for using his time in New York, his complete flexibility around my work schedule, his total availability, his lack of plans at Christmas. His devotion from the outset to his long-lost third cousin once removed. What can I say? I was distracted.

Mickey insists that falling in love with me was never part of the plan. But he also insists he fell hard, like a ton of bricks (an obscure Irish expression, he thought, charmingly, that I might not know). Never mind that it started as a complete setup.

"Forty-one, Patricia. I can't believe it at all. Look at you. You've been sealed up in some kind of cryogenic storage. In West Cork, the women have no teeth of their own by forty-one, they have chin whiskers, their dugs are down to their waists, they've dried up completely," he said. "When I thought to look up me fancy New York cousin, I never thought I'd be gattlin' after you. I thought you'd remind me of me mam, or me granny, or Sister Margaret from school. She was a terror, that one."

These remarks, uttered on our third or fourth night together, might have offended me had they not been murmured by Mickey as he lay sprawled in my bed, idly tracing a line down my bare hip with one intoxicating fingertip.

I *had* been in cold storage, until Mickey. How can I explain what it is about him? How can I describe the attraction in words? It feels so primitive at times that I am almost afraid of it—it, my desire for him, my obsession. Mickey has changed me. Everything has been rearranged.

Years ago, I saw a television documentary about heart transplants that fascinated me. The donor heart, which has been kept on ice, is warmed up and placed inside the chest where the diseased heart had been moments before. After hours of surgery, the moment of truth comes when the clamps are removed and blood flows into this new heart, which has been chilled and still for several hours. Warmed by the circulating blood, the heart slowly begins to do what a heart is meant to do—it starts to beat again.

Some of my best early memories are of sitting on my father's lap with my head against his chest, leaning against him, not content simply to listen to his voice travel through the air into my ears but also loving to feel it vibrate all through me as he told Irish stories—history and legends and folktales and family myths all jumbled together. Pete told me about Brian Boru. I was lulled at bedtime with the Battle of the Boyne. At seven, I learned about Michael Collins and the wars with the Black and Tans and the Easter Rising, all in one long night when I was up with the misery of chicken pox. I was forever being told about my own blood, the Dolans and the O'Driscolls. I can't remember a time when I didn't know about the Great Hunger, the terrible famine that began in 1846 and was utilized by the British to rid the Irish landscape of my ancestors.

I learned about the playful, magical side of Ireland as well, about fairies, ring forts, Celtic gold turning up under farmers' plows, the way stone circles and standing stones sprout on the misty hills like toadstools. I tried to believe that Saint Patrick really did lead all the snakes away. I learned that part of being Irish is having a deep relationship with history writ large and small. We rarely forgive, and we never forget.

And from my father I learned how it is that for the Irish, beauty and sadness and greed and bravery and passion and cruelty must at times go together.

And then Mickey came along. How can I find the words for what this is for me? Not only ordinary lust, not only loneliness and opportunity made this happen, though those things were part of it. Mickey has come to me out of the blue as the living embodiment of all of

Pete's ideologies and mythologies. How could I resist that? Why would I even want to? And the sex is astonishing.

My father's great-grandfather, one Michael Dolan, left the West Cork village of Leap—that's about eight miles from here on the Skibbereen road—at age twenty to escape the famine. It was 1848. He landed in Canada and settled outside Halifax, where he was a reasonably successful farmer, married a local girl (named Margaret Daly, or Bailey, depending on which records you trust, origin unknown) and had three daughters and one son. My father's grandfather Vincent Dolan also married a Nova Scotia girl, Maureen O'Driscoll from Sydney, whose father, Joseph O'Driscoll from Skibbereen, had sailed from Queenstown (Cobh, today) on the same coffin ship as Vincent's father.

They had six children, four of whom perished in a flu epidemic in 1907; only the oldest children, twins, survived. My grandfather Paddy Dolan was called up to fight for England on a French battlefield in the Great War, while his younger brother Teddy—younger by ten minutes—stayed home to work the farm. Paddy came back with a war wound and a pregnant war bride, my grandmother Rose Thornton, an English nurse who thought she had married some approximation of a prosperous Yank.

This match was not acceptable to the Dolan clan, who did not make them welcome. Teddy, who would never have gotten himself into a mess with some tart of an English Protestant, was given the farm. (In the end, he died a lonely bachelor, and what was left of the farm was razed twenty years ago for a housing development. Teddy's will—surely he was holding up his end of some soul-crushing deal with his parents—left everything to the Catholic church.) Too proud to stay, Paddy and Rose sailed immediately for Boston, where my father, their only child, was born at the height of a brutal heat wave in a third-floor walk-up tenement in South Boston. It was 1918.

Soon, Paddy found a few familiar faces among the Irish community, and after some menial jobs, he eventually became a policeman—truly a Paddy on the beat, though his brogueless Canadian "ehs" were a peculiarity. Rose never got over the unexpected hardness of her life. She more or less took to her bed—into which, it would seem, as they had no more children, Paddy was rarely invited—for the rest of her life. Rose Dolan died of heart failure when my father, Pete, was still in grade school. She had stopped living long before. My father doesn't often speak about his mother.

"Her death was only a relief, not a sadness, but the end of a sadness," he told me once, on a long car trip to Maine, where we would stay a week with my favorite friend of his, a retired detective named Jimmy Leary, a bachelor who had inherited his family's farm in Hallowell.

I was fourteen that summer. I hated my unreliable body and I hated the popular girls who possessed the secrets of the universe, or at least the secrets of eighth-grade success. I wished I were a boy so I could be the son I thought my father must have wanted, instead of my faulty female self, who perhaps reminded him of his mother, and, inevitably and more to the point, of my own missed and missing mother.

The way he said that about Rose's death, with a grim matter-of-factness, I believed him—I believed that he believed that the sum of his feelings on the subject was contained within the boundaries of those words.

"I never felt loved by her, only blamed," he said after that, shaking his head as if to clear it of further bad thoughts before turning to me with one of his let's-change-the-subject-shall-we head tilts and asking me if I would be ready for an ice cream stop in Damariscotta.

We would never have had such a conversation, brief as it was, if Paddy had been along with us that day. "Spare your granddad further grief on that subject," Pete always admonished at the conclusion of any conversation about his mother, though I needed no reminding. I always knew that the subject of Rose was off-limits around Paddy.

When he wasn't drinking, my grandfather was a big-hearted man whose love and kindness were nearly enough for my father as he was growing up. Paddy cooked and cleaned and kept Pete well, though surely the two of them were lonely much of the time, in that house without a wife or mother.

Paddy had been sent into exile by his own parents, he had witnessed the carnage at Belleau Wood, and he had failed to provide a mother for his son. While Paddy didn't seem to dwell on the grief in his life, those nightly tipples of Jameson, neat, must have been necessary to take the edges off the darkness.

I loved Paddy. I was named for him. When I think of him in my childhood, I picture him in his uniform, never civvies, though he retired when I was little and he must have stopped wearing blues. He lived with Pete and me at the end of his life. He was huge, had a loud voice, and an "abouwt the houwse" accent. He died of a heart attack when I was in junior high school. He had an enormous policeman's funeral. Bagpipes.

Pete has probably waged a lifelong battle with depression, to put it into clinical terms. The Dolan doldrums. How I admire my father for his strength, his decency, his struggles, his rages. Until now, my passions, if they could even be called that, have always been more cerebral, even when life seemed good. Maybe feeling too much of any-thing, even in the good times, would have been danger-ously close to missing my mother. In the more recent bad times, I have gone through long stretches when I don't think I can get out of bed and get dressed and pass for a person even one more day. Death does that.

In the last three years, I have accepted living in a permanent state of anesthesia, a highly functional but sealed-over kind of detachment. My hundreds of hours chipping away in the therapy mine have alerted me to some of what that's about, as well as to the power of my identification with Pete. No wonder I wanted to be a boy. But while I think I've gotten over most of my difficul-ties—or at least come to terms with them, worked through them, as they say in the terrible and distant lan-guage of the mental-health profession—my beliefs, my commitments, those things connect with Pete in a vital way.

And they connect with Mickey. I am, after all, here in Ireland, now, living out the Dolan destiny.

Sometimes I study her for so long that I need to get away from that room, and I go for a walk along the cow path that passes by the cottage and goes around the hem of the cove and up the opposite side. At the edge of a field where the cow path doubles back, I like to climb through a barbed-wire fence that's there to keep cows in, not the likes of me out, and then I walk across a series of crooked ancient fields toward the sea, all the way to the rock at the top of the cliff. That rock, or maybe the whole top of the cliff—I'm not sure which—is called Ardnageeha, which means "the height of the wind."

The Dutch painters of the seventeenth century were not afraid of the wind. Think of those skies filling the canvas; think of those towering dark clouds, those wind-lashed trees. At Ardnageeha, I imagine Jacob van Ruis-dael beside me, working with his characteristic probity, painting the wind's portrait.

21st of January, clear and cold

————

THERE ARE principally two kinds of conversations that have brought out the rages in Pete: when, as a provocative teenager, I unwisely pushed him a few times into further explanations for the cruelty of his father's parents, and the occasional shouting match he still gets into when some hapless person (not me, never me) voices the wrong sort of opinion about the British in Ireland. Or the British in China, or the British in India, or the British in North America, or the British in Africa. All through the Nixon administration, my father could go on for hours blaming the British entirely for the war in Vietnam.

When Pete gets the wind in his sails on the subject of the famine, there is no stopping him before he has denounced and damned the Brits to hell and back for their calculated genocidal policies. When I was growing up, I seriously believed that everyone knew that the two most evil men in history were Adolf Hitler and Lloyd George. When I said this aloud, my ninth-grade history teacher laughed at me. That was when I discovered that the world isn't always going to agree with the Dolans and that it is necessary and prudent, at times, to keep one's views hidden.

Do we need to do this now? There's a change in the air, maybe, with cease-fires that keep getting broken and put back together. Maybe not. I have so much to learn. Mickey has been very patient. There's a change all right, with copper-fastened coalitions and new brooms sweeping clean and people sitting down at the same table in the same room and all that. But there will be no selling out this time. Peace at any price is no peace at all. And we can't just sit back and wait for the once and future Little England to get it together. They have had their marching season and now we will have ours.

We won't wait. We are not waiting. They've been standing on our necks for too many years. The past is always present, as Mickey says. We must never lose sight of that.

My biggest regret, my only regret, is that I can't tell Pete what I'm doing, what this is about. I think he would be proud. I hate to lie to him, and I wish I didn't have to, but Mickey has given me no choice in the matter. Oh, Pete. I know he'd be proud.

Perhaps every generation of every family has its own myth of the lost fortune. My grandmother Rose's disappointment, so the story goes, was about being cheated out of certain prosperity. At least that's where her sorrows supposedly began. Though who can say what the first part of her life was like? We hardly begin to know all of her baggage when she sailed for the New World. She was an orphan, a brave and plucky battlefield hospital nurse, according to Paddy, according to Pete, so she must have had a fair amount of courage and gumption. She should have been able to deal with the comparatively tame adversity of those pigheaded Dolans who balked at welcoming an English girl into the family, hinting darkly all the while about who knew for sure if the bun in the oven was one of our own or some Tommy's leaving.

Whatever its source, her bitterness was profound. You could say she squandered her own good fortune. My father has spent his life mourning that loss, that missing love. Sometimes I wonder if he would have such violent opinions about the Brits if they hadn't been the source of his own troubles as well as Ireland's.

Until his mandatory retirement some twelve years ago, Pete was, inevitably perhaps, a detective with the Boston PD. He lives in an apartment on O Street in

South Boston now. For a few years, he worked part-time as a guard at a bank, though, with his pension, he really didn't need the work. He was a formidable presence, even in the bogus uniform of the security service. Pete spends most evenings at Foley's, an Irish bar in Southie where they speak his language.

I think one of the reasons Pete took that security job was the uniform, which kept him connected to his youth, his days in the navy during the war and later as a rookie on his first beats. The Dolan men look good in uniforms. He started out in Dorchester, then transferred downtown before he made detective grade and began to dress in the plainclothes uniform that he wore throughout my childhood—khaki pants, a white button-down shirt, and a threadbare tweed jacket, with a rarely worn necktie looping out of one of the jacket pockets the way a doctor's stethoscope hangs out of the pocket of his lab coat.

I suppose this inventory of Pete's wardrobe makes him sound professorial-looking, but when I was a child, two things kept him from resembling my friends' fathers, who were mostly academics and lawyers: his shoes, spit-polished black wing tips, and the way his jackets always fit badly over his gun.

My mother died when I was five years old. She was thirty-one when she died of breast cancer. When I think of her, I don't know that I really remember her so much

,

as I remember missing her. My clearest memory is of her hands.

She must have been sick, near the end, in bed, perhaps sleeping while I sat with her. I don't remember her speaking; I can't remember the sound of her voice. Perhaps it was the last time I saw her. I don't know if it was five minutes or an hour that I spent with her that day. Or maybe my memory is faulty and I am conflating several different occasions into this one, crystalline image. I have a soundless recollection of bright sunlight and shadows slanting across a window ledge, and the smell of freshly laundered sheets over another smell— the odor of stale water in a vase of dying flowers, or death itself.

But my strongest memories are almost always visual. When I think of her, I think of that day, and when I think of that day, I recall the contrast of her yellowish skin against the white of the bed linen, her hands like bird wings, skimming the covers, a gesture I would recall with a shock of recognition twenty years later in front of a van der Weyden in Munich, at the Alte Pinakothek.

My own hands, I discovered that afternoon—surely the light I remember is afternoon light?—were miniature replicas of hers, yet the skin on mine was new and perfect-fitting, and the skin on hers was loose and fragile. Very gently, I pinched and squeezed little tents of the pliable folds that covered the bones on the back of her hands while she slept. I matched one of my hands to hers, laid it on top of hers, pushed my five fingertips into the corresponding whorls on her knuckles.

Then she wasn't there anymore and what I remember of her after that is only her absence.

She was Louise Kelly from New York. (Her Kellys are probably the Kellys who emigrated from Mallow, also in County Cork, just at the end of the famine in 1851.) I don't know very much about her family. Her mother was a Gross from Bridgeport, Connecticut, possibly Jewish. I never knew my maternal grandparents; they retired to Arizona when I was a baby and then they died, unexpectedly, one after the other, before I was eight, leaving me some very useful money in a trust. Grandpa Kelly had been a fireman in Queens. I have no authentic memories of them that are not based on a couple of bleached scallop-edged snapshots of two white-haired people holding a tiny newborn me on their laps.

My parents met at a Saint Patrick's Day party in Boston, to which my mother had been brought by a guy with whom my father had served in the army. The story goes: Who's the pretty girl? my father asks his buddy. I don't want you to meet her, his buddy replies. Why not? asks my father. Because, his buddy says, if I introduce you to her then you'll marry her.

My mother taught the fifth grade in the public elementary school I later attended. Though it might have been the obvious thing to do, I wasn't sent to parochial school. In our house, God was certainly respected, but not feared. Pete called himself a collapsed Catholic, and especially with few grandparental pressures—Paddy never brought it up—we rarely went to church. Christianity interests me as the subject of so many of the world's great paintings, of course. Beyond that, it occurs to me right now that I have always thought of myself not as a Catholic but as an Irish Catholic. I do try to get to Mass on Christmas Eve and at Easter, though I'm not quite sure why. I think it's because I like the smells, the odor of incense and true faith that comes wafting off the older people. I like the ritual, the rhythms of it, as much as the meaning of it. The largeness and smallness of each moment.

The way I miss my mother, the idea of my mother, will probably be with me for the rest of my life. But it's entirely Pete I've been thinking about since I got to Ireland. I feel very much that it's Pete Dolan's daughter tramping the road into the village, here at last in the land of her forebears. Not that Pete's ever been here. For all the talk, he has never set foot on this island. We never traveled any farther than Maine or Cape Cod for a couple of weeks every summer. I grew up, yet another lonely only Dolan child, went through the public schools, and spent my first twenty years entirely in the Mission Hill neighborhood of Boston, just across Huntington Avenue from Brookline, Massachusetts, birthplace of Saint John Fitzgerald Kennedy.

But right now, as connected as I feel to every rock and furze bush in West Cork, it is deeply frustrating to me that I can't tell a soul in Ballyroe that I have O'Driscoll blood. I have managed to produce a vague, uninterested smile when more than one person has mentioned to me that I have the look of a Dolan all right, that there are Dolans in Skibbereen, Dolans in Timoleague, Dolans down in Red Strand, Dolans in Clonakilty, not five miles from here. I'm sure there are, and I'm sure that more than a few of them are my cousins.

So is Mickey. (His great-great-grandfather James O'Driscoll was my great-grandmother Maureen O'Driscoll Dolan's brother; they were Skibbereen O'Driscolls.) How can it be that I've known him just weeks, since the middle of November?

But I've always known him. Mickey is the light of my life, the fire of my loins. Michael Patrick O'Driscoll. He is only twenty-five years old and I am forty-one—not quite Humbert Humbert, but this is a little shocking and I am a little shocked—and I am greedy for him.

◙

Thinking about him changes the way I am breathing right now. I am blushing, alone in this room, in this cottage at the edge of nowhere. Have I lost my mind? Is he just some atavistic fantasy of my own devising? Have I dreamed up this halcyon Irish interlude?

I've certainly thrown over my traces. I am alive again, reinvented. I exist in the world in new ways because of Mickey. This was meant to be, if anything was ever meant to be. That sounds melodramatic. What would be better words for this? Mickey O'Driscoll has asked me to come here and I have done it.

Sometimes people do the right thing for the wrong reasons.

In my heart of hearts, I cannot say that I am as committed to the cause of uncompromised and everlasting freedom from the Brits as I am in love with Mickey. Would I be here if anyone else had approached me two months ago and appealed to me on purely ideological grounds? Truthfully, probably not. But maybe. I'll never know.

I do know that I believe with all my heart that the British government has no right in Ireland, never had any right in Ireland, and never can have any right in Ireland. The presence of the British government in Ireland is a usurpation and a crime.

Those are more or less the words of James Connolly, who commanded the Dublin Division at the General Post Office attack that began the Easter Rising in 1916. Because he was wounded in the fighting, he was propped up and tied to a chair for his execution by British soldiers. Paddy gave me five dollars for memorizing Connolly's words when I was ten, and he used to delight in trotting me out for a recitation when the precinct's floating poker game landed at our house.

If my performance came late enough in the proceedings—that is, after the beer and Irish had been flowing for a while—it would usually elicit tears and shouts and lots of maudlin singing.

I am, either way, as deeply certain of the rightness of our plan as I think Pete would be, if he knew about it.

"I think I'd like yer old man. A tree is known, after all, by its fruit," Mickey said when I quoted to him over our soup on that first afternoon the basic Pete Dolan rant on the subject of Charles Edward Trevelyan and the obscenity of the so-called Relief Commission, which presided over the genocide we call "the potato famine."

Of course, much depends on the treeness of the tree, I told him, and he laughed.

There is a love for the real, an affection for the true, in all of Dutch art. A church interior with its stillness. A hand with its gesture. A landscape with its distances. A cloud with its motion. People being people. Dogs being dogs. Cheese being cheese. Sky, always, the sky, conferring proportion and context on everything. But there is always intimacy, the intimacy of experience without pretension.

There is a profound link, for me, between Irish passion and Dutch restraint, here on the edge of the sea, in this cottage alone with her, in all her radiant serenity.

22nd of January, foggy, rainy, sunny

———

I FIRST VISITED the Isabella Stewart Gardner Museum on a class trip in the sixth grade. I was stunned, shocked by the existence of this place. We were led around by a harassed-looking fortyish woman who was called a "docent"; because I had never heard the word before, she seemed exotic to me, decent and docile and intelligent. I was thrilled that this woman seemed to exist to provide me with information about the paintings. And I didn't just love the paintings; I loved the idea that the paintings were so important that a magnificent villa had been erected to house them all.

The docent had us on a high-speed elementary school schedule, and we traipsed from one end of the building to the other, stopping only when she had something to say about certain paintings that someone had decided would interest schoolchildren. My classmates jostled one another, shuffled their feet, fidgeted, whispered, and were clearly bored, but I was mesmerized, transfixed, enthralled.

"Sometimes you can learn all sorts of things about people when you look carefully at a painting, children," the docent implored above our murmurings. "Can anyone tell me something about the people in this painting?" She indicated the picture in front of us, which was Vermeer's *The Concert*. I had never seen anything like it. What art there was in my household was not very interesting—the most appealing item that I can remember on the walls was a free calendar from the bank that reproduced twelve Currier and Ives prints.

Here was a new world. I drank in the complications of light and dark on the carpet on the table. The wall glowed with reflected sunlight. I had an overwhelming desire to be in that room with those three people. There was a landscape painting visible inside the raised lid of the harpsichord and another on the wall. What possibilities! I could hardly take in the life that was indicated by this painting, the promise of life. The love of the real. I felt effaced by it, absorbed.

I was suddenly impatient that the figure of the man sitting on a chair in the middle of the group, in the middle of the canvas, blocked my view of the hands of the woman seated at the harpsichord. I wanted to see her hands. Someone made a rude sound behind me, and there was muffled giggling. I heard the word *fart* whispered.

"Anybody?" the docent chirped desperately. She caught my eye and nodded at me. I felt my face go hot. The docent nodded again. I felt the other kids looking at me. I looked at *The Concert*, desperately trying to find words.

"There are three people in the painting on the wall, just like the three people in the room," I began, hesitant. She nodded, encouraging me. "The man sitting with his back to us"—I realized now he was playing a lute, and was part of the concert, not just an audience—"his hair is dark, like the man's hat in the painting inside the painting. It's like when a word rhymes with another word—it's like a rhyme, kind of, the way the different things in the painting go together," I finished lamely. The docent smiled at me. The other kids began to laugh. Tears sprang into my eyes.

I wasn't crying from embarrassment, I was crying because I found the painting so moving. I decided I wanted to be a docent when I grew up. I think it is reasonable to identify this moment as my very first act of art history scholarship.

After that, I spent so much time at the Gardner that most of the guards came to know me by name. Pete gave me a big book of paintings by the Dutch masters for my twelfth birthday. I liked the landscapes and the still lifes, but I studied the paintings of interiors with a deep certainty that those still rooms held something for me—a marvelous sense of serenity and comfort and completion. I felt so loved by those paintings.

Somebody's at the door. Nora O'Driscoll.

To be continued—

Later, afternoon

————

THE COTTAGE on the Rock, some locals call it. It belonged to old Denis O'Driscoll, who died two years ago at eighty-nine, the last of three bachelor brothers who lived their entire lives there—the two other brothers and a sister married and moved away—and it has been rented out to the occasional extremely intrepid tourist only a few times since his death, while his various nieces and nephews (one of them Mickey's uncle) squabble over who owns what percentage of it and how to get the most money out of the place. It will go to auction once the dust settles, Mickey says, but that could take years, even with the assistance of somebody who knows someone in the Land Registry.

These five small rooms must have been cleaned up a

fair bit since Denis O'Driscoll died—I noticed evidence of a recent bonfire out in the field; there is something touching about the twisted remains of rusted bedsprings in the middle of the ashy heap. The cottage is austere but reasonably comfortable. There are two "electric fires"— that is, electric heaters—and the fireplace throws heat well, now that I have finally mastered the science of getting a turf fire going with nasty-smelling fire starters. My second morning here, Nora was appalled that I had started a fire with bits of twisted willow branches I brought in from a walk. She says it's bad luck.

The upstairs three rooms have been painted white, and though furnishings are sparse, the bed is new, as are some of the rough sheets and towels. There are some ancient sheets that are soft as velvet, but they have uncomfortable, lumpy Frankenstein's monster stitches where they've been patched and mended. The downstairs floors are rough concrete, poured, Mickey told me, over dirt floors only a few years ago. There's a rumor that the O'Driscolls were in the habit of burying gold coins in various corners of their cottage and that there is a hidden fortune buried here still.

There is absolutely nothing on the walls, which makes me notice the scraped creamy pudding of the walls themselves, immensely thick rough plaster. The only upstairs windows are at the gable ends of the cottage, and each has a sill almost two feet deep. The middle, windowless, room is really more of a closet, with built-in cupboards on both sides. I keep my clothing on one side. The gray Samsonite suitcase, when it arrived, fit perfectly on the cupboard shelf on the other side.

Electricity is a relatively recent thing, run into the village in 1964, according to Mickey. The O'Driscoll brothers pumped water from their well by hand into the cistern in the attic, and they relied on bottled gas for their hot water and their cooking.

The cottage was finally wired for electricity not quite six months ago. They didn't exactly go wild with it. The only light in each room is a single bare bulb, but I've gotten used to that, just as I've become accustomed to the strangeness of electrical outlets that have to be switched on, making toast under the gas grill, and drying my tub-washed laundry on the fireplace fender, which infuses my clothing with a not-unpleasant smoky smell of peat. (But I had never before appreciated the softness that tumble drying confers on sheets and towels.)

There is scalding-hot water, though not much of it, and it's hard to get in the habit of planning two hours ahead for a bath (there's no shower). I keep forgetting the little switch on the wall for heating an entire tubful of hot water; otherwise, there are just five gallons of near-boiling water ready for dish washing or anything else. When I commented on the awkwardness of this arrangement to Kieran O'Mahoney, he nodded in agreement, saying, "'Tis awkward all right. Many's the time when I thought I wanted a bath, but by the time the water was heated, I found I'd lost the urge."

I have learned to use a dishpan, to stop running all my hot water away washing dishes under the running faucet. What an abstemious country this is, I think at times; but then, what a wasteful country I come from, I think more often. Mickey told me that, as it happens, it was his brother Sean, who works for O'Donovan in Skibbereen, who was sent out to install the copper electric hot-water cylinder just the day before I arrived.

A feeling of Denis O'Driscoll is still about the place in myriad ways; on the mantel, there's a briar pipe with charred tobacco still in the bowl, holding down a stack of curling religious postcards (all sent by Sister Ann, whoever she was or is, from a pilgrimage to Knock, a devotional shrine north of here, in 1989), and there's an old walking stick, its bent handgrip worn smooth, by the door. Burn marks fleck the scrubbed top of the kitchen table at one end, probably from pipe embers. The two knives in the kitchen drawer have been honed so many times that the blades have worn away in a tapering curve.

There's a wooden settle in the room Nora O'Driscoll calls the kitchen, which is to say, it was the kitchen in the days when all cooking was done in the fireplace, and now it's more of a sitting room. The settle is like a church pew, but the bottom is a hinged box and opens into a bed, of sorts. When I opened it, I was surprised to find a stained and narrow old blue-and-white-striped mattress, so it has been used for sleeping in recent times.

Apparently, people used to hide in these settle beds. Though it seems obvious enough, Nora has told me with great drama that the Black and Tans didn't know that they opened, and when they raided a farmhouse in pursuit of someone, if there was an old granny peeling potatoes in the corner on the settle, who would expect to find a fugitive or two beneath her?

Perhaps Denis slept in the settle at the end of his life—he might have preferred the warmth of the fire, and he might not have wanted to climb the steep stairs. Living in this cottage, I have begun to feel that Denis O'Driscoll must have been a methodical man, and a kind man, though I may be romanticizing completely. It must also have been a fairly harsh and lonely life. An old black bicycle stands where Denis left it, against the wall inside the shed that holds kindling and sods of turf for the fire. The bicycle's front basket is an amazing object woven from the remains of a donkey basket, plastic fertilizer bags, baling twine, and fishing nets.

There's a sincere yet pointless thrift everywhere I turn, from a collection of little lengths of baling twine saved from the fields and hedges that hangs on a nail in one of the little falling-down outbuildings, to a drawerful of screw tops from bottles of Power's and Paddy's and Jameson.

There's an ingenuity, as well, in the thoughtful way a nail has been lashed with baling twine to make a latch on the shed door. The old ladder hanging in one of the sheds has rungs fashioned out of old soap boxes; if you look carefully, you can piece together an antiquated Fairy Soap logo. There's something very beautiful about the Mondrianesque arrangement of driftwood boards fitted together on the ground like paving that Denis or his brothers fashioned to smother the weeds by the kitchen door. Pete would love this place. I think of him all the time, and I keep feeling at odd moments as if I'm here for him, as if he could see it through my eyes.

The celebration of domestic virtues in Dutch genre paintings honors these sensibilities. But there is everywhere here an Irish wildness in the crags and bluffs and boreens, perhaps a disordered wildness that the O'Driscoll brothers tried to defend against with their methodical arrangements. The flatness of the Dutch polders, all those fields of tulips marching off in soldierly rows to the horizon, that order and symmetry—surely, those straight lines contributed to the Dutch way of seeing, the Dutch way of describing.

I would have liked to have known the O'Driscoll brothers—the lads, as they are still remembered in the village, though they all lived well into their seventies and reputedly had long white beards. Kieran O'Mahoney told me that from the time he was a little boy he knew of them, but glimpsed them only rarely. They did things the old-fashioned way, he said with respect in his voice, they eschewed modern convenience at every turn, wearing traditional jackets and neckties and caps every day of their lives. They were my second cousins twice removed, I think. An extremely close tie, when I consider it.

The lads never went down the two miles I walk nearly every day into the village. Not once in the past thirty years. Only Denis would venture beyond their own pastures to walk as far as the now-defunct creamery for a few supplies now and then. They were "shy." Which is to say, they were practically hermits, but no one would judge them for their eccentricities, or maybe the difference is that they were not merely tolerated; they were respected. Their kind, and apparently there are a few more scattered about the countryside, are dying off, never to be replaced.

A cottage like this, perched on the edge of this unspeakably beautiful cove, will soon enough belong to a rich American, or German, or, at best, a Dublin Yuppie. After I spent my Kelly inheritance on my education, I never imagined that I would have serious money in the bank someday. The money gives me freedom, but I hate it because of what it represents and so I rarely use it, and so it sits and grows. I give away a lot, anonymously, to charities that help children, usually. I meet for about an hour with a lawyer four times a year and decide how I want the money used. But maybe, someday, I will take some of that blood money and buy a cottage like this. Would I want to live out my days in a place like this? Maybe yes.

And then there's the very lean marmalade tomcat with an enormous cabbagey head who glares at me from under the fuchsia hedge beside the door. Tiggy is his name, according to Nora O'Driscoll, the farmer's wife from up the road who keeps the key to the cottage. Much of my information comes from her—I get milk, eggs, and potatoes from her, and we have an easy ability to slip into a few minutes of conversation each time we meet. With very little prompting on my part, Nora has provided me with a great deal of local history. I imagine that talking to me beats talking to herself.

Nora is pyramidally huge, but seemingly built of solid muscle under many grimy layers of farmer's clothing. She does the work of a man. I have no sense that her husband and sons help very much with her cows. They're always off doing something in some remote field, unless they're spreading exceptionally noisome slurry, which they seem to do exclusively in fields directly upwind of me.

I've only glimpsed Nora's husband, Pat, from a distance, on a tractor. He's a dour farmer, hardworking but a bit joyless, according to Willy, the postman. The O'Driscoll sons are indistinguishable to me, big farm lads between the ages of sixteen and twenty-two, with red faces under their pulled-down caps; they're called Liam, Vincent, Joseph, and Connie.

She was no relation to Denis, Nora insisted on telling me as some obscure point of order, or pride, at our first encounter, offering an elaborate (nearly insane) explanation of the "upper O'Driscolls" and the "middle O'Driscolls" and the "lower O'Driscolls" and which are which in the village. (Of course, ultimately, they're all related. Nora is undeniably some kind of a cousin to me, as well.) She identified the cabbage-headed creature as Denis's cat when she let me in the morning of my arrival.

"Get away, Tiggy. Get away off the ditch!" she commanded out the window over the sink as she was showing me how to light the old gas stove (she calls it "the cooker"), when he flattened himself on top of the wall as if to spring in through the kitchen door. (Adding to my confusion in my first days here is the way people call a wall a "ditch" and a ditch a "dike.") Tiggy's gone wild just lurking around the cottage these past two years, poor loyal thing, rather than find another home. Denis died very unexpectedly, I learned just today from Annie Dunne, who was, I think, trying to spook me.

"You're above in Denis's place, missy. He was found floating on the tide, you know," she said not two hours ago, cocking her head vaguely in the direction of the cove.

"Some say he threw himself in, but the official verdict was accidental drowning. Maybe a heart attack, maybe a fall, but definitely a drowning. He was alive when he went into the water, they could tell that much—'twas drowning killt him all right."

She had waited until the only other customer, an old woman from the village in a moldy black overcoat, who always nods to me and mutters, "Dirty weather!" by way of a greeting, had paid and left before she imparted this nastiness. I didn't want to give Annie the satisfaction of a reaction and so was silent, thinking that I had been right to sense her malevolence. This was definitely my last visit to her shop. (How hard could it be to bake my own scones, anyway? I must ask Nora for her recipe.) She had rung up my total and I had paid and was halfway out the door, unsettled by this information (about which Mickey has told me nothing), when Annie added under her breath, "Some say he was thrown off the cliff above. Or pushed."

"Why would anyone murder an old man?" I countered. I didn't want to get into it in any depth with her, but I was startled and somehow irritated, defensive. I also felt a little deceived, kept in the dark by Mickey, and not for the first time. I stood in the open doorway and waited for her reply, knowing the cold draft would annoy her. People here are obsessed with avoiding cold drafts.

"He was original IRA, you know," Annie hissed. She has some very long chin whiskers, which occasionally glint in the light. "Some say he knew about the ambush. Was involved, like."

I shrugged as if this meant nothing to me, my heart racing, and stepped out into the wind, trying not to look rattled. When someone in West Cork says "the ambush," only one thing is meant by it: Beal-na-mBlath, just a few miles from here, where Michael Collins was murdered in 1922 by his own people, who turned on him as a traitor for signing the 1921 treaty, which left the six counties of the North under British rule.

Is Annie Dunne a madwoman, or could there really still be retribution and infighting about the treaty that would lead to the death of an ancient original IRA member, all these years later? I don't suppose I'll ever know whether or not Denis O'Driscoll was involved with Michael Collins's murder—it's possible, but he would have to have been a boy, a lad—even if he was actually involved in the IRA at all, though it wouldn't surprise me. I wish I could talk to Pete about this. He'd have some good detective's thoughts, and he'd be intrigued. Mickey probably knows, but he wouldn't tell me if I asked—that much I've learned. The only truth I can know with certainty is that this is the sort of thing people say to one another in the village of Ballyroe on a weekday morning in January.

Tiggy subsists on handouts from the farms along the road—old Mary Carew up the lane is his principal benefactor, I'd guess—and hunts down the occasional mouse or rat or baby rabbit, as well. There are plenty of rabbits. That first morning almost three weeks ago, I went out the kitchen door to talk to him and he flashed away under a hedge. Having sorted me out, Nora was in a hurry to get back up the road before her husband and sons were in from the fields ("time to get the dinner") and she asked me to come back into the cottage to see her out the front door, because she wouldn't leave by the kitchen door. She seemed shocked that I didn't know what bad luck it could bring if you exit a house through a different door than the one you entered. She was shocked again this morning, by my recidivism, I suppose, when she saw me at the edge of her field gathering some fallen willow branches to use for kindling.

"'Tis always bad luck to burn willow for warmth," she admonished with exasperation. "Surely they know that in America?"

More than one of Denis's nephews borrowed money from him habitually, according to Willy Hayes, the postman, who brings me a letter from Pete every few days. Willy is young and bright, and he always seems to have time for a good chat, leaning in the doorway out of the rain, the motor of his little green An Post delivery car running. He might be flirting with me, but I really don't know that. When I asked him the other day how he can possibly deliver the post in a village without street names, populated almost entirely by people named O'Mahoney, Hayes, and O'Driscoll, he simply laughed uproariously, a high-pitched Cork trill, as though I had made an exceptionally funny remark, though I was serious—I'd really like to know how he does it.

Yesterday, when Willy handed me a letter from Pete, he said, "Here's a little reminder of yer real life," and I found myself replying, "No, *this* is my real life. My real life is here. Now."

Willy also had a separate packet of forwarded mail from Pete—bills mostly. I can hardly believe that the phone company and Con Ed and all the rest still click right along, unchanged. It's as if my life is going on back home without me.

I don't miss my work. I thought that I would. I love what I do and I'm very good at it. Being a research librarian means that I never know what century I'm going to be working in from one week to the next. Essentially, I assist scholars with their work. In those hectic days of making the plan with Mickey, at the library I was focused on finding sources for researching the clothing worn by Fragonard's subjects, assisting a professor leaving for Venice with a study group on material for his Bellini lecture, and helping an architect find the material she needed to re-create a room originally designed for

Madame de Pompadour. Dr. Calabresi, the chief librarian, who hired me, said that I was ideally suited to the job, knowing, as I did, "something about everything, and everything about something."

Wanting the visit with Willy when he called this afternoon, yet suppressing the more pointed questions I would have liked to ask him, and still smarting from the conversation with Annie Dunne, I inquired if Dunne was a local family.

"Enniskeane way," he replied, shaking his head vigorously to indicate that they were most certainly not the least bit local people at all (Enniskeane is perhaps twelve miles away), and then he added, with a conspiratorial giggle, "You've had the treatment, have you? Some bit of rudeness or cuteness? Then you've been done. That's what we call it. You've been done, all right. Pay Annie Dunne no mind at all; she's a right gligeen, that one."

Those so-called loans to impecunious nephews (I really do hope Mickey wasn't part of that crowd) are why most of Denis's land was sold off over the last years of his life to supplement his pension and keep him going. Now the cottage sits on a hapless rhomboid lump of land, a small weed-choked acre, vicious nettles mostly (allegedly worthwhile in soup, but I would need rubber gloves just to pick them), surrounded by cultivated and well-tended fields belonging to the neighboring farmers who bought those fields one by one.

I was lonely here, the first week, with not much to do. I missed Pete. All this Irishness, all this Ireland! And though he knows I'm here, he thinks it's just a romantic interlude with Mickey, with maybe some *Roots* kind of curiosity, as well. (*Spuds?*) It pains me that I can't discuss the plan with him. It's so hard for me to lie to Pete that I've just barely kept him informed in the vaguest ways of my whereabouts and plans. It's such an unusual state of things between us that I am worried that he'll think I'm mad at him for something, but I don't know any other way to handle it.

My mail is being forwarded to him for sorting out, and he's written to me a couple of times, but we're oddly polite and distant with each other right now. I suppose he's giving me my privacy with Mickey. And I know he's happy for me, after the past three years. Katie's death was a terrible blow to him. He never speaks of her. Oh, we Dolans know how to be sad.

So in that first week, I could only settle in as best I could, write carefully to Pete, find my way, find myself a little bit. I spent hours just sitting in the cottage, reading the books I had brought with me—William Trevor short stories that seem to be set in this very village, my favorite Iris Murdoch novel, *A Severed Head*, and some Walter Benjamin essays that seem to be about everything in my thoughts right now.

In "The Work of Art in the Age of Mechanical Reproduction," Benjamin writes:

Katharine Weber

Even the most perfect reproduction of a work of art is lacking in one element: its presence in time and space, its unique existence at the place where it happens to be. This unique existence of the work of art determined the history to which it was subject throughout the time of its existence.

24th of January, overcast, drizzle, fog

––––––

ALONE, IN the cottage, waiting, I feel as though I have been coming to, waking up a little more each day. There has been something almost hallucinatory in the clarity of my thoughts. Maybe it's the landscape. Maybe it's thoughts about Mickey, about us, though we haven't talked about the future, about life after this is over. I have made such a leap of faith.

I have never been more alone with my thoughts than the time between the day I arrived here on the sixth—Epiphany—and the day the painting arrived, on the sixteenth. I am so conscious of sound here. In New York, I suppose I am constantly filtering everything out. Sometimes in the cottage the wind blowing across the chimney top makes a constant roar. Other times, it is so quiet,

I can hear Nora's cows crunching grass in the field when I walk along the hedges.

I haven't been in the mood to write in this ledger daily. And I have to keep it hidden, because while I have never been specifically so instructed, something tells me that a written record would be completely out of the question. It would have been stupid to ask permission about keeping a journal, after all. (Even when I was little, Pete used to encourage me to make decisions independently. Instead of asking his permission—for things like swimming alone in Maine, or climbing on the roof of our garage—he urged me to consider the request from his point of view. Anything that I knew he would say no to was something I probably shouldn't consider doing.)

In that first lonely, uncertain week, I found a secret hiding place of Denis's, under the stairs. Don't ask me why I was poking around under there with all the spiders and filth. A board dropped away on a primitive rusted hinge when my sleeve caught on a protruding nail, revealing a very small, shallow built-in cupboard shrouded in sooty cobwebs. There was a huge old-fashioned key to some long-gone lock, and a rusted tobacco tin with about fifty disintegrating one-pound notes inside. I've left the tin where I found it.

I don't think single-pound notes are in circulation anymore, only big pound coins with a deer on one side and a harp on the other, so the tin has been undisturbed for a long time. Maybe Denis knew nothing of it—it occurs to me that this might not have been Denis's stash at all, but that of one of his brothers. Or it could go back further than that. The pound notes look big to me, bigger than the notes in my wallet, so they may be quite old.

I'm satisfied, anyway, that in recent times no one has noticed the existence of this under-stair cranny. As a way of camouflaging my hiding place for this diary, I've taken to storing firewood and sods of turf in a heap under there, so my comings and goings, if I am somehow observed, should arouse no suspicion.

Looking over these pages, I see I'm straying badly. This isn't art history; this is autobiography. This is meant to be an account of what, exactly? The lesson of *The Music Lesson*. Sam, my ex-husband, always accused me of being unable to stick to any point whatsoever, and he wasn't wrong.

"Just tell us the details," he would say, glazing over with impatience, a phrase he picked up from a cute utterance of our five-year-old daughter, Katie, who had, of course, meant precisely the opposite.

I knew I would get to this sooner or later. Life is not fair. If life were fair, Katie would be alive and Sam and I would still be together. They say very few marriages can survive the death of a child. It's true. I would add that very few individuals can survive it on their own. I didn't think I had survived it, until now.

A school bus. Rain. A driver who looked but didn't see.

Very small consolation: There's a new law on the books in Connecticut, Katie's Law, requiring safety devices on the fronts of school buses, making that sort of accident much easier to prevent. When the bus is stopped for loading or unloading, not only does the STOP sign swing out to the side to stop passing traffic but also a yellow gate unfolds off the front of the bus, preventing anyone from walking too closely under the front windshield, just below the driver's line of sight.

I can't describe this safety gate without considerable pain, because each time I have happened to see one in use, it looks to me like nothing so much as an animated diagram of what happened that afternoon in the third week of kindergarten. The bus stops. The lights flash. The arm swings slowly, like a pointer—*She was walking just here*, it says, stopping for a long moment to indicate the location of fatal impact before it sweeps back to fold up against the front of the bus like an insect's wing.

I don't live in Connecticut anymore. I didn't want her name used for the law, but Sam persuaded me to allow it. I don't even drive now, not that my driving had anything to do with it. I was a good driver, actually, but after the accident, I lost my confidence. I became afraid I might hit something or someone and not even know it. I let my driver's license expire last year.

So I don't have a car here, which is awkward, but so far I've managed, the worst of it being the bus ride from the airport in Cork to Clonakilty, the bus from Clonakilty to Ballyroe, and then the trudge up to the cottage with my bag. A farmer gave me a lift on the back of his tractor for the last mile, though I hadn't asked for one. He's Billy Houlihan. (His mother was a Hayes, Willy told me. Billy is his cousin. Of course.) Billy gives me a jaunty little two-fingered salute whenever he sees me out walking on the roads. I always feel that we have some sort of connection, because he was my first Ballyroe inhabitant.

"All on yer own, is it?" he asked me that windy afternoon in the watery sunlight, appraising me frankly. The countryside is teeming with lonely bachelors. Billy might be thirty and he might be fifty.

"Divorced," I replied, though he had only meant to ask if I was on my own in a literal sense, now that I think of it. I'm still not sure if my being divorced is a turnoff (it's a sin) or a turn-on (she's got some experience).

"Oh, well then," Billy replied, blushing.

Most of the people I have come to know since Katie's death—I've loads of acquaintances, but I have developed no intimate friendships—know I used to have a husband, but they don't know I had a child and lost her. It rarely comes up in conversation. It rarely comes up in my thoughts. No, that's completely wrong. A lie. I have learned to tune it out because it is so constant in my thoughts—like tinnitus. I have been in such pain for these past three years that I have learned not to have feelings. Or at least that's what I thought until now.

I couldn't stay in that house, in that life, in that state. It wasn't Sam's fault. Katie's death killed something between us. Maybe we didn't have a great marriage anyway, though we'd been together for nine pleasant years. It surely killed something in me. New York doesn't have a Katie's Law. In Manhattan, the school buses aren't equipped with the gate, the moving diagram of how a child might die. Though I prefer not to look at school buses under any circumstances, anywhere, if I can help it.

There's something else I cannot bear to look at anymore: the Metsu painting *The Sick Child*. Before I was a mother, the subject matter didn't have any particular meaning for me—I could study the way it was painted, the light falling on the sick child's pallid skin, without feeling anything particularly. Then Katie had a terrible virus when she was three, and her fever soared to 105 through an exceptionally harrowing night of cold baths and the fear of convulsions, and all that night my thoughts kept going back to that painting, because it seemed so true to the experience of holding a feverish child. Since Katie's death, the painting seems to me to be about death. It's so clear now, inevitable, that the child is going to die. How could I have never noticed that?

There was so much money. Insurance money. What does it insure? That the heartbroken will go away rich. The city of New Haven cannot make this up to me. They cannot "cover" this "liability" with dollars. I have not been "protected from loss" by money, any more than sending my child to kindergarten was a "reasonable assumption of risk." I wanted Sam to keep it all, but he persuaded me to divide it, and in the end we did.

The money hasn't changed my attitude toward my work, the way I thought it might. I worried for a while that I could drift without the necessity of earning a living. But I find that I am doing what I want to do. I work hard, but at the same time I don't have to think about my lost income while on unpaid leave from the Frick, or worry about paying the monthly rent for my apartment while I'm away. I will never again have to think about running up the phone bill, or paying for plane tickets, or buying a really nice pair of shoes.

There was a time—not so long ago, when I think about it, but it seems like another life—when I thought I might have to go into private dealing in order to pay for Katie's education. When she was an infant, I even had a couple of lunches in New York with different dealers in old masters who wanted me to work with them. It's admittedly a nice thing that I can afford to do the work that matters to me without fretting over my meager salary and benefits.

I was the number-two person in the art library at Yale, which helped me to get my job at the Frick Art Reference Library. They're pretty flexible about my schedule, since they don't have to pay me when I'm not there.

Having very few close friends has made it disturbingly easy for me to slip my moorings. I left a message on my machine that I'm on a trip, which won't surprise the odd friend who might be looking for me. I've told my colleagues at the Frick that I had an urgent family matter to deal with and I didn't know when I would be back, and no one was interested enough to ask me much about it, so I didn't even have to use the lie I'd worked out about a sick relation in London. If it weren't for Pete, and aspects of my work, I would have very little reason to go back.

Sam has done better at getting on with his life. He still has his architecture practice in New Haven, and, last I heard from a mutual acquaintance at the Yale British Art Center, his work goes well and he has a serious girlfriend—a divorced woman with a little boy. I'm glad for Sam that he could go on living in our life when I couldn't. It was a good life. He's great with children, and I'd like to be happy for him, but it tears my heart. It really does.

We named her Katie because when I was about six months pregnant with her, Sam woke me in the night to tell me that he had dreamed that our baby would be a girl and that I was insistent that she be named Katie Cathexis. (Sam was in his sixth year of psychoanalysis at the time. I wonder if he's finished yet.) It seemed hilarious, but then it stuck.

We gave her a different middle name, of course— Ellen, for an aunt of Sam's. Katharine Ellen Hodgson. She was a wonderful baby. Sometimes I would hear Sam singing to her in the night, when she was colicky or teething and it was his turn to be up with her, Katie Cathexis in the deep blue sea/Swim so wild and swim so free—

No. I can't do this. Not even now. I have to stop.

Later. It's crashing with rain. So much for drizzle and fog signifying that it won't actually rain, according to that great weather predictor Kieran O'Mahoney. I have spent the past hours up in the small windowless middle room where she must be locked away from the world, contemplating her again. I can join her in that simple, peaceful chamber, with the rich afternoon light falling through the window across the wooden grain of the table, the glazed surface of the gleaming white pitcher, the soft, precise fuzz of the peaches on the windowsill. The sun has warmed the smooth black and white squares of the stone floor. The lute lies in her lap, under her fingers. Her gaze has a steadying, hypnotic effect; with her, I feel safe. She connects with something in me. The smile that isn't quite a smile. The knowingness, the intelligence—they're generous gifts across the centuries. Nothing is more real, not the view out this window to the sharp little islands that have broken off this ferocious coast, not my own hands holding the pen moving across the page. Her presence dazzles me. How could Vermeer have made her up?

She must have lived, I have to believe that there was an actual woman possessed of this sensibility who lived 330 years ago. And lives in the present, made immortal by the greatest painter who ever lived. What I can't quite reconcile, given my art history training (Smith, then Mt. Holyoke—my thesis was a consideration of the relationship of Cubism to the still lifes of three seventeenth-century Dutch painters) is my own refusal to know that I am responding to a painted image.

I confound myself with the feeling that this painting is merely a representation of something actual. While intellectually I can accept that this is indeed illusion—that I am in the presence of the genius of Vermeer—I am simultaneously convinced that she lived and she still lives, brought to life and kept alive on a painted panel.

Which is, incredibly, here in the room with me, alone in this cottage on the edge of Gortbreac Cove, in Ballyroe, County Cork, in the Republic of Ireland, on the western edge of Europe, in the world, in the universe, and so on, as Stephen Dedalus would have it. *What was after the universe? Nothing.*

25th of January, sunny and clear

————

I WONDER HOW I would judge me. I mean if I were told about a woman doing what I am doing, I wonder, What would I think?

As an outsider, I would say at the very least that this woman is playing with fire.

That's what obsessions do for a person. I am in the grip of a fine synergistic madness. I am in a fog of lust and I am the true fruit of the Dolan tree in my hatred of the British in Ireland and my belief that I am taking part in an action that will help move us closer to a solution. Many people would say that I am not in my right mind. I'm certain that's correct. What a relief, I say. I look back on three numb years of being in my wrong mind. In front of me is an unknown future, but it's something very bright and very hot, like the sun. So pardon me if I don't mind the danger. I'm skimming over the ground now, faster, weightless, rising, barely touching the treetops. Soaring higher. Higher.

27th of January, blustery, raw, dark, awful at
the moment

———

T
HE WEATHER has been very wild, with a few sunny
intervals, as they say on BBC longwave. The always
moving sky always moves me. The always changing
weather produces incessant rainbows. At home, a rainbow is, almost by its very nature, kitsch. But an Irish rainbow isn't one of those anemic little colorized wisps.
These Irish rainbows are a full 180 degrees' worth of spec-
tacular showmanship on the part of God or the Irish
Tourist Board. From here, it looks as though the pot of
gold must lie on Red Strand, just past Galley Head.

The first time I glimpsed a rainbow, on my second
morning waking up in the cottage, my impulse was to take
a picture, to regret that I had not brought a camera with

me. What is that? A basic American imperative to seize and record foreign experience in order to take it home, own it, consume it? Here in this cottage, among these simple necessities, I don't like that impulse. I reject it.

Having rejected it, at moments when I experience the drama of changing light, or happen upon an extraordinary view, I can just look, or turn away, as it suits me, having gotten past the wish to possess it all on film—in these days here, I've lost the urge. I'm traveling light.

A photograph can convey a false authenticity, a last word in experience and knowledge. This is what it looked like at this moment.

What would Vermeer have made of photography? It's been debated for centuries that he may have employed a camera obscura in his work. My own view is that he was a genius who was capable of recognizing and appropriating the "objectivity" of the camera obscura, which is not to say that he literally projected camera obscura images and traced them in his work, as some have suggested.

Vermeer was original—he did not need the camera obscura. Why can't people understand that? Because he had seen camera obscura images, Vermeer saw things in new ways, which led him to paint in new ways. I cannot abide the art historian's way of concluding, that smug "aha" that signifies only information, not feeling for art. Like this century's Dutch master de Kooning, Vermeer was a "slipping glimpser."

I wonder if Vermeer could have ever anticipated a time when photographic images would themselves be considered works of art. Maybe he would have been thrilled by the possibilities of technology. I like to imagine that Vermeer would have recognized how cameras create new ways of seeing, but it would have been as a means to some further inspiration to making paintings.

Walter Benjamin wrote, "The technique of reproduction detaches the reproduced object from the domain of tradition." He wrote about the aura of objects, and called it "the unique phenomenon of a distance, however close it may be." He wrote about "the desire of contemporary masses to bring things 'closer' spatially and humanly, which is just as ardent as their bent toward overcoming the uniqueness of every reality by accepting its reproduction."

I look at the painting and it takes my breath away. She does. I forced myself to meet her gaze this morning, to hold it, and then I started to cry, flooded with the feeling that I wasn't seeing; I was being seen. *So this is what it is to be known.*

I wonder what Vermeer would make of the way we prize the authenticity of photographs, much the way autobiographical writing is more popular than fiction these days, because it claims to tell of actual experience.

But what is the "real" truth of anything? Vermeer's woman conveys her own reality in her grace, her strength, her nobility, her beauty—they are human traits, surely, but Vermeer has applied them evenly to the room, to the objects, to the light itself. It's a love of the real expressed on a thin slice of oak, in paint, some 330 years ago.

What is painting but the art of expressing the visible by means of the invisible? It's made up. It is a product entirely of the human mind. A mind has meditated to conceive it, and minds must meditate to understand it.

I had a message from Mickey this morning. I've settled into routines, and the short hours of sunlight dissolve the days into fleeting intervals between long, dark nights. I was taking a walk up a tiny rutted boreen to nowhere that loops around above the village, past some crooked little farms. My favorite local character, Mary Carew, a Scot by birth who has lived here most of her life, has the last place on this road, a tiny pink cottage. We talk about all kinds of things when we meet.

The first time I passed by her yard, I couldn't believe the number of cats about the place—up on the windowsill, under the hedge, lying on the top of the wall, sitting in the doorway. Mary came out the door just then with a pan of milk for them (or perhaps she was curious about me). Her white hair was coming loose from its old-fashioned mooring in a swirl on top of her head, she wore a generous smear of bright pink lipstick that went well beyond the upper and lower margins of her lips, though it didn't quite cover the corners, and she looked slightly crazy to me. I asked her how many cats she had—there were easily a dozen in plain view.

"Oh, I can hardly say it to you; I'd be ashamed for you to know" was her answer, in an unexpectedly high little voice, like a child's. She's nearly eighty, widowed since the war. Her husband, George Carew, had spent summers in the cottage, which was in the family because he had an Irish mother, a McCarthy from Tipperary. Late in the war, George Carew was shot down over Germany. They had no children—they were just married, living in a flat in London, when the war began. Mary has lived in Bal-lyroe since the war ended, in the place where George spent his childhood summers. She's got almost no family, just a nephew of George's who married an Irish girl and lives on a farm near Myross Wood, beyond Union Hall, just a few miles from here.

From that first encounter, we've developed an almost-daily habit of a little chat. And Mary has, finally, in a show of confidence, revealed to me that she has twenty-eight cats. Tiggy, she has told me, comes from her farm. I know I'm supposed to keep my distance from people so as to avoid calling attention to myself, but Mary's not Irish and we never discuss politics, so it seems like a harmless little connection. If anything, my visits with her might allay suspicions on the part of the locals that I'm so solitary, I must be up to something. Mickey is paranoic, I say, if he really believes that talking about cats and books with an old Scottish lady up the lane could doom our enterprise in some way.

And I'm a little lonely. Other than almost daily encounters with Nora, who obviously feels responsible for me, and is also probably proud that she has me to look after, and my little bits of conversation with Kieran O'Mahoney in the shop, my chats with Mary are a welcome diversion.

She's amazingly well read, I blurted out to her yesterday at the end of a rambling chat in the shelter of her chicken house doorway. We somehow got onto a Margaret Kennedy novel I had read as a kid, only because it was misshelved next to *Profiles in Courage* in the downtown branch of the Boston Public Library. Mary had just finished *A Constant Nymph*, having found it in the little library in Clonakilty, which she frequents when she does her shopping. She drives an ancient Morris Minor for errands, though she loves to walk.

"Och, Patricia, the telly's so depressing, newspapers are depressing and dear as well, and there's not much else to do with myself but read in the dark of winter, with my garden put to bed until spring." Mary sighed, the closest to complaint I've heard from her. "You're a treat to have around for the odd chat," she added, hugging herself in her shapeless gray cardigan against a sudden wet gust. "Though who's to say when you'll get the wind up your tail feathers and be gone."

She's offered me cups of tea, but I keep refusing, because then I'd be in her house, sitting by the fire, and that might be dangerous.

Compared with the locals, Mary's unusual in her tolerance for personal exposure to the weather during our chats. She's probably considered eccentric, and she is, of course, an outsider; she goes to the Protestant services in Union Hall or Clonakilty. I get cold and wet nearly every day, which makes Nora think I'm "daft as a brush" and likely to come down with pneumonia or at least some sort of nineteenth-century fever. I suppose if being dry and warm were a precious state, one difficult to achieve, then a person would become obsessed with preserving and maintaining it. I have always lived with the luxury of hot water and the certainty of a warm and dry change of clothes. And I don't know what it is to grow up without those things.

Sometimes I bring carrots in my jacket pocket for the three shaggy donkeys that are always standing together in the top field no matter what the weather. I don't know whose they are or what purpose they serve. Sometimes all three are stoically and stupidly facing into a raw wind that's spitting ice pellets. Those ice pellets really hurt. And there I am, up there with them, not knowing any better, either.

I'm not supposed to leave the cottage for more than a couple of hours at a time, nor should I just hang around all day long. Mickey has been very specific about this. I would get restless to the point of distraction in this transcendent landscape, and, more to the point, lurking indoors exclusively could itself attract some attention and speculation about my motives for showing up out of the blue and renting the O'Driscoll cottage.

So tramping around the countryside a bit seems true to form as an activity for your basic oddball single woman having a tame adventure. I play the part perfectly. As I make my rounds, dogs bark at me, some unseen person in the farmyard or kitchen speaks sharply and commands the dog to stop its racket, and the dog wags his tail and follows me for a bit; in that way, I have come to learn the name of nearly every dog this side of the village.

While the dogs have names—many collies seem to be called Lassie, for instance, and there are numerous working dogs called Shep and Pup; there's a Bruce, and a Joker, and a Beauty, and there's Benson, a fat old black Lab named after an American television program that starred a black actor some years ago—the cats rarely do.

Mary's cats are an exception. They all have names out of Shakespeare, though it gets confusing when a kitten called Hamlet has Goneril for a mother and Othello for a father. It's all mixed up now, but originally, years ago, the Lears started out orange, while the Macbeths are the original black and whites. (Tiggy's mother was a pretty gray tiger called Juliet; Mary thinks his father was the old black one-eared tom she calls Shylock. She doesn't care for the name Tiggy, but she couldn't persuade Denis to call him Falstaff.)

I've not gotten beyond ordinary discussions of weather with any of my other neighbors. Sometimes when I meet a cat on my walks, I stop and have a conversation with it, and sometimes this leads to a friendly chat with the farmer's wife, who has been attracted by the unfamiliar sound of my voice—or by the barking dog. When I ask for the name of a cat, more often than not, the farmer's wife will reply, "Oh it has no name—it doesn't come into the house."

The roads have no names, either. If everybody on the road already knows where he is and where he's going, then I suppose in this thrifty country there's not much point in wasting effort on signposts. I have no idea if people call these roads anything, even informally, if the roads have the equivalent of nicknames. God only knows how the fire truck finds a burning cottage. God only knows if there is a fire truck.

◻

On this boreen without a name, there was a Telecom Eireann van parked at the side of the road, with a Telecom guy up a pole, fiddling with something, a fairly ordinary sight. Especially in the winter winds, there are always problems with telephone and electric lines. The electricity was off for several hours at midday yesterday, which I didn't notice until I heard a generator humming in the distance at the Hayes farm on the other side of the cove. I have no idea if telephone service was affected as well, because, like most of the people this side of Ballyroe, I'm not "on the phone."

So I thought nothing about the Telecom van, nothing at all. The air was very still, for a change; it was an unusually bright morning, though the sky was white with high clouds, and I could see him a good distance away, across several fields, as the lane winds around—so he was intermittently in my view and then hidden by dips and rises and then in sight again. I had been out walking perhaps forty minutes. There was no one else in evidence, though the sound of a distant tractor engine sometimes can echo as if strangely near, bouncing off the water in the cove from across the fields.

The landscape is so open here, scraped bare of the forests that grew hundreds of years ago. The eye accepts these contours as what the west coast of Ireland looks like, but I am reminded of Pete's quoting a British lord of the eighteenth century: "The Irish will never be subdued so long as there are leaves on the trees."

What was meant by that was simply that the native population of Ireland couldn't be controlled so long as there were forests to hide in, that destroying the trees was part of a strategy for keeping the Irish from finding protective cover in which to organize themselves. But it occurs to me now that a completely contradictory interpretation of that remark would be this: There will always be leaves on trees and the Irish will never be subdued.

I was walking. The perpetual delicate morning mist that threads together with the thin smoke of peat fires lay across the low spots, concealing and softening everything ever so slightly under its gauze.

As I got nearer to the Telecom man, perhaps half an hour after first having him in my view, he came down the pole and stood by the open back door of his van, rummaging in a parts bin. Just as I was passing by, he said in a low voice, without turning or looking up at me, "Mickey says to tell ya that he'll be down to ya next week. Say nothin'. Keep walkin', for feck's sake. And next time ya go out, do a better job lockin' up the windows. The upstairs bedroom on the west wasn't closed a'tall."

He had what I have come to recognize as a Northern accent—almost like Mary's Scots buzz, but clipped, without the heathery edges, and all his sentences went up at the ends in a flattened, rhetorical tone.

I shouldn't have been surprised, I suppose, but I was deeply startled. Again. Each contact with Mickey's people is surprising. This was the third communication that has come at me out of the blue. It makes me feel both protected and vulnerable.

On my eighth day here, there was a grizzled pensioner outside O'Sullivan's Pub who dropped a note into my pocket as I passed by on my way to O'Mahoney's. The note was an unsigned instruction to wait for a telephone call in the one telephone booth—call box—outside Nolan's Pub in Ballyroe at noon the following day.

And two days ago, I was walking in the cove at low tide and thought nothing much about a woman picking mussels off the rocks. She had a dirty-looking long skirt, patterned like drapery material, black farmer's wellies, and a shapeless coat, and her head was wrapped in some sort of snood against the wind. She looked to me like a tinker, or "traveler," as they are properly called, one of the gypsyish people, perhaps from the controversial encampment on the Bandon road. (The local newspaper is full of articles about the county council's plans to erect housing for them. Then they would become something actually called "settled travelers.")

After perhaps twenty minutes of my sitting on a rock in the sun while the woman moved slowly in my direction, she worked her way closer to me, until she was beside me, and then she slipped me a Ziploc bag with an unsigned note from Mickey from the bottom of her bucket of mussels. The note said, "Contact made. We've got them by the mebs now."

What I want to know is this: How could the Telecom man—this whatever, this operative, who may or may not actually be employed by the telephone company—have known that I would walk that way just then, when I didn't know it myself until I set out? He probably knew how many carrots I had in my pocket. I must ask Mickey about this. No, I mustn't. I wonder what day next week?

Mebs are balls.

28th of January, foggy

———

I MYSELF have been in a fog for weeks. From mid-
November to Christmas, I think I drifted around the
library at the Frick in a dreamy postcoital stupor most
of the time, somehow managing to do my work.

I've been adrift on a sea of sex. I've been awash in a
flow of feelings. I've been ahum like a tuning fork next to
a crashing grand piano. I've been a glorious wreck.

It isn't Mickey's fault. How could it be his fault that
something about the place on his right clavicle where
there is a faint spray of freckles makes me feel a harsh
thump of excitement? Each time I see it. Or think about
it. It isn't his fault that the sight of his slightly blunted
thumbs makes me flush when I think about the way they
know me. And how could it be his fault that his penis—

his "willy," such a friendly, gentle term—feels as good as it does when he enters me, especially that first slow thrust as my wet flesh gladly yields to receive him yet again?

I had never seen a foreskin before. No, that's not true—Max from the play group was uncircumcised. I was quite startled the first time I changed his diaper and encountered his little carrot. Mickey's foreskin is my first adult one. It's fascinating, watching the swell of blood and the emerging glans like a blossom unfurling in daylight. It's touching, inspiring.

I, who have been unfazed and uncharmed by most of what life has arranged for me in the way of company, found myself moistening when we lingered over espresso in the café two blocks from my apartment on that second night, when we knew we were going to be together. On the walk back after dinner, I registered such engorgement, such desire-swell, that I remember marveling at the discreet design of a woman's body.

Perhaps it showed on my face? I wondered, stopping to peer into a shop window at my reflection. I saw only the face I knew, and beside it the face of the man whose clavicle, thumbs, and soon-to-be-met parts would render in me this apocalyptic effect on a continous basis.

Glazed with desire, that's what I have been, like some erotic pastry. I'm all at sea; can this be love?

My intention has been to tell this story the way it happened, but I haven't exactly begun at the beginning. Perhaps the real beginning was on a particular night in late December, after weeks spent mostly in bed together (not that it matters, but, for the record, we didn't actually go to bed until after dinner on the second night—though I am embarrassed but not ashamed to admit that I think I had maintained a state of continuous sexual arousal from that first touch across the table at E.A.T.). Mickey said one evening that he hoped I could give him some advice about paintings.

"What about paintings?" I said dreamily, the tip of my tongue twirling the tiny golden hairs that surround his left nipple. He took my chin gently in both his hands and lifted my mouth away from his chest. It was three days after Christmas, our first night back in New York. Mickey and I had taken the train up to Boston to spend Christmas with Pete. We dragged in a too-large tree for him, and when we ran out of ornaments from the box Pete still keeps from my childhood, we decorated the rest with popcorn and cranberry strings. Mickey was incredibly nimble at stringing the popcorn without breaking it, his deftness like that of a surgeon, though he swore he'd never done it before.

Awkward and wary at first, Pete and Mickey had rapidly become so delighted with each other that I had begun to feel superfluous. Mickey has a kind of easy grace that often makes me forget that he is only twenty-five. He has an old soul.

What is Mickey like? I don't know. When I try to think of him in specific ways, he evanesces. Intense, funny, kind in an incredibly sexy way, sexy in an incredibly purposeful way. Pete was probably very much like Mickey when he was young.

The first night, when I saw Pete bring out his precious Red Breast, a vintage Irish whiskey he rarely shares, I knew Mickey was in like Flynn. (Who was Flynn, anyway? Some charming Irishman or other, no doubt.) They stayed up talking and drinking until three or four in the morning. By the time Mickey finally came to bed I was sound asleep, having read until the book—my dog-eared high school copy of Maugham's *Cakes and Ale*—dropped on the blanket a few times, and I had finally given up and turned out the light.

They did it again the second night, and though I was beginning to feel neglected, there was something quite wonderful, too, about the intensity of their affinity. I fell into a peaceful sleep, listening to the low murmuring of the voices of the two men I love.

It was the first Christmas since the accident when I hadn't felt so lost and alone that all I wanted to do was lie comatose until after New Year's when I could go back to work.

"I want you to pick one out," he said, looking at me with sudden seriousness. "Could you do that?" It was about seven at night, which is to say, we had come in after a day of drifting around the city (Brooklyn Museum, South Street Seaport, World Trade Center) and we had torn our clothes off and gone straight to bed without stopping for food.

Generally, we would wander out onto Amsterdam Avenue afterward, starved, and eat dinner in one of the small places in my neighborhood, or bring something back. We had fallen into this routine almost immediately. Occasionally, when I was at work, Mickey would have started to cook something by the time I came home. These were very happy days. Needless to say, Mickey never did spend very much time in Rego Park.

Which is not to say that in our intense little storm of mutual discovery in those weeks we didn't find time to talk, to talk about, oh, everything: movies, books, Mickey's skills and ambitions with fine cabinetry, his love of sailing, my love of art, my work, arguments about the best temperature at which to drink beer, preferences for breeds of dogs, Chinese food, the virtues of sleeping with window shades up or down, Irish politics, stories of childhood adventures, my stories about Pete (with whom he had chatted cautiously on the telephone a couple of times before they met)—all the usual getting-to-know-you conversations. (Though, as I have said, it emerged later that Mickey, through his mysterious sources, had already gotten to know my particulars.)

Now, with that deepest evening darkness of late December pressing against the windows, we lay twined together like satiated kittens.

I eyed him and put my head back down on the bony indentation below his sternum.

"What do you mean, pick one out? One what? A painting?" I listened to the quiet steady thump of his heart. "There's one over there," I said languidly, pointing to the framed poster from the Matisse in Morocco show that hangs on my bedroom wall. "It's very blue, that painting. Very Moroccan. Very Matisse." I wasn't really paying attention yet.

"What I mean is, on a purely theoretical basis, if I showed you a group of paintings, would you automatically know which one was the best?"

"Oh, Mickey, of course, sure. You bet. The Patricia Dolan prize for excellence is awarded to...*this* one." I reached up and pressed my fingertips to his philtrum, which is perfectly formed, like that of a Raphael angel. His lips parted a little, and I slid my index finger down and slipped it between them. We were like children, always touching, always playing. He welcomed my finger with a brief touch from the tip of his tongue, just for an instant, but then he pushed my hand and turned his head away, suddenly serious.

I tried to answer him more fully.

"Every art historian of whom you ask that question would say yes, but the real question is, Would any two art historians pick the same painting? People have their biases. And isn't it ultimately about taste, anyway? It would depend on the art historians, and on the paintings, and probably on what the art historians had for lunch that day."

Mickey laughed a frustrated little yelp and rolled over, away from me, dumping me onto the sheet beside him. I felt him tense up in some subtle way. I touched his shoulder and he didn't say anything for another long moment.

"Mix? I'm sorry I laughed at you. I'll try to be serious. Is there something you want me to do? I don't know what you're asking. Do you want me to look at somebody's paintings and give advice? Somebody at Simon's workshop? You know I'm not very good on contemporary work. I haven't a clue about the gallery scene."

"Do you think," he asked in a measured voice, very slowly and deliberately, keeping all of his consonants rounded up instead of letting them blur at the edges, "very seriously, Patricia, given your expertise in Dutch paintings of the seventeenth century, that you could pick out the best Vermeer from a group of paintings that are all by Vermeer?"

"Are you kidding? You mean, go to The Hague and see the Vermeer show with you, something like that? I think you've missed the boat; it's closing after next week. The time to see it was when it was in Washington."

I rambled on about the Vermeer show, not really noticing the direction of Mickey's questions. I told him a long and semipointless story that had been told to me by an acquaintance who works at the National Gallery about the President touring the exhibition, unscheduled, and how some two thousand ticket holders—eight hundred an hour was how they were scheduled for that show; just think of that, all those people so anxious to have a glimpse of those twenty-three paintings—had been kept waiting by the Secret Service for two and a half hours because the President had shown up that morning unannounced, with a sudden need for culture.

"Do you have access to special privileges in The Hague because of your Frick connection?" Mickey asked abruptly.

"Not especially. You know we wouldn't lend any of our three to that show, which is very typical of the Frick," I answered, still thinking we were talking about what we were talking about. "It's too bad, for lots of reasons. Our paintings are important—well, any Vermeer is important—but at least two of them should have been included simply from a scholarly viewpoint. And on a more practical level, there would have been the possibility of some courier assignments coming and going to The Hague for Frick staff, and it would have been a lot easier for all of us to get tickets to the exhibition, too.

"You and I looked at the Vermeers when I was showing you through on that first afternoon, remember? Before we looked at the Fragonard room. *Officer and a Laughing Girl* with the soldier and that big dark hat? *Girl Interrupted at Her Music* was almost next to it. I don't like her face at all—it's too weird, flattened, almost squashed. I'm sure he was getting at something, but it doesn't work for me. Our best Vermeer, the *Mistress and Maid*, is in the West Gallery, in with some of the Rembrandts. It's the last painting Henry Clay Frick bought before he kicked the bucket, not that you'd need to know that."

Mickey was nodding impatiently and making a one-handed spooling gesture that was either a signal to keep on as I was or a request to hurry it up and get to the details. I tried to return to what I thought we were discussing, which was my having seen the Vermeer exhibition in Washington.

"I told you then that those Vermeers were skipping the family reunion in Holland, remember? It would have been unconscionable for me to miss the Vermeer exhibition, even if the Frick was sitting it out. So I flew down to Washington on the shuttle to see the show just for the one day, a couple of months ago. I had a VIP pass for the morning, before the public viewing began. I really hate Washington. Everything feels so governmental. It was a madhouse of people clutching VIP passes, and afterward I positively craved those delicious little Dutch pancakes, *poffertjes*, which I ate the one time I went to the Maurits-huis, the summer of my junior year in college. Have you ever been in Holland, Mix?"

"You've already seen all the paintings? The same paintings that are in The Hague right now? At Maurits-huis?" Mickey sat bolt upright and peered down at me intently, as if my rambling disquisition on the Vermeer show suddenly was the most utterly wonderful and origi-nal set of remarks anyone had ever made to him. He didn't answer my question.

"More or less. You pronounced it wrong—it's just like *house*, not *hwees*. How did you say that—*hwees*? I like that. It sounds Irish when you say it."

He ignored me and persisted. "You've seen all the paintings, then?" I was still puzzled by Mickey's fasci-nation with my every thought about the Vermeer ex-hibition.

"I think that there were a couple of paintings that didn't travel to both shows—maybe not every Washing-ton picture that was stuffed into the show regardless of current thinking was invited to The Hague. Maybe there were a couple of pictures from Dutch museums that were shown in The Hague that hadn't been especially wanted in Washington. Traveling exhibitions usually work that way—I don't remember the details of this one. So, literally, maybe not, but yes, basically, I've seen the Vermeer show. When did you get so interested in Vermeer, Mickey? You didn't seem too fascinated by the ones at the Frick—you actually said you preferred Chardin to anything else in the collection. Actually, your favorite thing of all was the tunnel from the library building to the collection itself."

He didn't answer me. He was thinking. Then he spoke, still not really answering me.

"Patricia, if you could have any single one of those paintings in the Vermeer exhibition, which one would it be?" A playful question asked in deadly seriousness.

"*The Music Lesson*," I said without hesitation, matching him for gravity, not at all sure where this was going. "Do you want to see it? I've got about fifty books with Vermeers in them."

Not waiting for his answer, I hopped off the bed and went out into the hallway, which is lined with floor-to-ceiling shelves for all my books.

"Here she is," I said a moment later, back with a big volume about Vermeer and his circle that I have owned since Smith. We sat cross-legged, naked together on the bed, the book on the covers between us.

"I haven't looked at this in a while." I reached past Mickey for my reading glasses on the bedside table. A few weeks earlier, I could never have imagined being on such casual and intimate terms with a man again. To think that I could sit this way, naked except for my reading glasses, unself-conscious of so many things—my forty-one-year-old stomach, my personal smells, my hair no doubt looking beddish and wild. I hadn't been alive in so long.

"I love this woman," I said after leafing through to find *The Music Lesson*. "I have always loved this woman. See? So, in answer to your question, I choose her. Absolutely the best. Look at that face. Look at those hands. Look at that sifted light. There's no yellow in the world like a Vermeer yellow."

"Not *Lady Writing a Letter with Her Maid?*" Mickey sounded a little plaintive.

"No. Certainly not."

"Reason?"

"No. Personal preference. You asked for the best. For my best. I like *Lady Writing a Letter*, but it just doesn't get me where I live."

Mickey was turning pages, as if he was looking for something. He found it. "How about *The Concert?* Do you think that was an important Vermeer?"

"My first Vermeer. Oh, God, I *loved* that picture. I used to visit it all the time when I was a kid. I've always thought it was a wonderful painting." I was so pleased that Mickey kept picking topics I know so much about! Teacher, teacher, call on me, call on me! I know the answer! "But of course it's not in the show. It disappeared in 1990—it was part of the big Gardner theft—so I wasn't thinking about it just then. *Was* might be right. Who knows if we'll ever see that painting again. I guess no one really knows what that was about."

Mickey tsked and murmured, "Someone must." He was leafing through the book, turning pages, squinting at the plates. I think he needs glasses.

"Well, sure, you hear strange rumors from time to time. There's a corrupt art dealer from Newburyport who claims to know something, but he's in jail now for fraud and wants a pardon before he'll talk. And there's another guy trying to save himself with a deal with the feds, too, an antiques dealer who says he knows something. There's a lot of buzz about those pictures from time to time, but who knows if anything will ever come of it? I filed a fascinating Interpol bulletin in the library about those paintings just last week. You know the reward is up to five million dollars now? Those were some terrific Rembrandts stolen along with the Vermeer. The last time I was there, it seemed so sad to me, the way the Gardner leaves the spaces on the walls blank, as if to exhibit the absence of the paintings."

"Wait. Stop." Mickey inhaled so sharply, I thought he was in some kind of pain, or had developed a cramp. But he was simply keyed up by something he had seen in the text on the page facing *The Music Lesson*.

"It says here that *The Music Lesson* is the smallest

known Vermeer, and it's on a wooden panel, not canvas. Does any of that affect value?"

"In what sense? These aren't yard goods, Mix. Vermeer was generally at his best with the intimacy of a room. Other than one of the early pictures, *View of Delft* is his biggest painting, inch for inch, okay? And it's extraordinary, and it's considered one of the world's most beautiful paintings—I've always thought that Swann's Vermeer obsession began with this painting."

Mickey didn't necessarily know anything about Proust, but I didn't stop to footnote. He was intently focused, his head cocked slightly to one side as if he was listening for some distant signal.

"But it's not the best of Vermeer, even though it's magnificent," I persisted, this being something about which I am unrelentingly passionate. "*The Little Street* is the only other painting that's not an interior, unless you count some of the early religious or allegorical pictures, which show some sky, but I'm not even considering those because they interest me the least. I think Vermeer lost control of the light when he left his rooms. *The Little Street* has some of the intimacy of pictures like *The Music Lesson*, but if you're asking me to pick a winner, your *Lady Writing a Letter* comes in second to *The Music Lesson* by a good length."

The language of horses is metaphorical for most people, but it happens to be one I know because Paddy used to take me to the races a lot when I was a kid and talk to me about handicapping.

What looks promising, sweetheart? he would ask. I picked them based on the names, usually, just names I liked. Paddy played wild hunches based on numbers. There were six birds on the fence, which had six strands of wire—so, the number six horse in the sixth. He won, sometimes.

Paddy would walk me to the window, teach me how to place a two-dollar bet, to which he would stake me. Nosey Mike to show at ten to one. Miss Berry Time to win at six to one. My first savings account was started with my winnings when I was about eight. I still sometimes like to take a peek at the *Racing Form*, just for the names.

I studied *The Music Lesson* awhile, absentmindedly taking in the odd tone of Mickey's questions, and rambled on.

"Of course, even if we wanted to hop on a plane, we couldn't see this particular painting for a while. There's no way in hell we could get tickets for the last days in The Hague—people at work were telling me just this morning that we couldn't swing it for one of our lots-a-bucks trustees who called from there to see if our director could pull strings. Every minute is spoken for—it's like the last plane out of Saigon."

"I'd like to see your *Music Lesson*," Mickey said softly.

"Not mine. The queen's, actually. Anyway, it usually takes weeks for pictures to get reinstalled after a loan show like that. There's a trip to the conservation lab to check condition, and some curators are big believers in 'resting' the paintings, if you can believe that. So it could easily be a month or two before *The Music Lesson* is back on the wall. How about it—are you up for a trip to London, maybe in the spring? She lives at Buckingham Palace. I think they let commoners in these days. They need the cash or something. 'They're changing guard at Buckingham Palace/Christopher Robin went down with Alice.' I'd love to go to London with you, Mix, and take you to the National Gallery. There's so much good art there. My favorite van Eyck."

Mickey didn't speak. Somewhat self-conscious about my tendency to ramble and instruct simultaneously, I stopped, and looked down into those eyes of hers again, studied that faint smile, the bemused air somehow also present in the hands playfully splayed on lute strings centuries old.

"Maybe she's friends with her neighbors up the road at the National Gallery, the Arnolfinis," I said, breaking the silence. More silence. "They both keep fruit on their windowsills." Mickey could not have known what I was talking about. Silence again.

We bent our heads and studied her together for a long time then. I held back on any little lectures on iconography or painterliness or Northern European sensibility or the hilariously named nineteenth-century art dealer Jeronimo de Vries, or anything at all, to let Mickey look at the painting through his own eyes and not mine. In truth, from then to now, Mickey has never indicated to me if he feels anything personal at all for this painting.

"So, *The Music Lesson* it is," he murmured after a while, as if to himself.

I could sense him looking at me thoughtfully as I studied the color plate in the book some more. I found that I was staring at it without seeing it, I became so conscious of his gaze. He was quiet for so long that it began to spook me, and finally I broke the silence, with a tease.

"Is this my next birthday present? I have to admit I was thinking a little smaller for you, Mix, maybe a nice plain Jaguar XKE. What color would you like? Green, don't you think?"

"It's worth millions, isn't it?" he said quietly, resisting my kidding.

"Well, millions, I guess, sure. Maybe hundreds of millions. Who's to say? Vermeers don't just come up at Sotheby's or Christie's. There are only—what, not even forty paintings known? Thirty-seven? Thirty-five? I never can quite remember which ones are in and which ones are out of favor. It depends on whom you talk to. Some very orthodox scholars count only about twenty-eight for absolute certain. I myself have a funny feeling that the girl in the red hat in Washington is not entirely quite right. That one's on wood, too. But the other little panel portrait in Washington, that girl with a flute, she's definitely got a problem. She's way too direct somehow, too enthusiastically present. More of a Maes kind of face, you know? No, of course you don't, but I can show you and you'll see it. She's had a major exfoliation or something in the last couple of hundred years, too, which hasn't helped. Though it's my sense that some of the questionable ones were unfinished at the time of his death, and then greedy people messed them around in order to sell them. That would account for what's right with them as well as what's wrong with them."

I sneaked a peek at Mickey to see if he was listening. He seemed to be, so I kept talking. "*The Music Lesson* has never been questioned, by the way, even though it's on an oak panel. It's the only absolutely definitely A-OK Vermeer on a wood panel. So, if anything, that might add to its value, I suppose. Its provenance is impeccable. Vermeer's widow sold it to a baker to settle a debt the year after Vermeer's death. It paid for bread. Isn't that amazing? This painting paid for bread for Vermeer's widow and eleven children."

I had been enjoying the feeling of letting my own expertise out for a canter, given Mickey's apparent fascination with my knowingness as much as with the subject under discussion. But I was suddenly self-conscious, feeling that I was sitting there naked, babbling, making a fool of myself, boring him.

"Just about every Vermeer is in a museum or public collection, anyway," I concluded. "So it would be impossible to say what this painting would be worth. How much is priceless on the open market?"

"Perfect," he breathed. "You are perfect, and she is perfect. And she's a Brit to boot, and she's owned by Betty Windsor herself, which is brilliance on top of brilliance. I am in love with you both."

Mickey leaned over and kissed the page, kissed the woman in *The Music Lesson* very softly on the edge of her face, and then he closed the book carefully and put it on the floor beside the bed and lay back on the pillows, pulling me with him. I tugged the covers up, suddenly chilled. He lay on his back contemplatively, with his hands behind his head, as if something momentous had been settled.

"Uh, Mix, does this conversation have any meaning?" I ventured after another long silence.

"This conversation will change your life," he said.

The first thing I did when I was alone with her—this is something I feel very strongly about and I am not afraid to admit this, though some would think that I risked injuring the painting—was take the panel out of the frame. I did it in order to remove the glass.

I hate glass. I cannot be more emphatic about it. I hate it. It's a recent trend in museum management, glazing paintings, because it's cheaper than hiring enough guards and it protects the merchandise—the work of art people glimpse on their way to the interactive CD-ROM installation—from vandalism or accidental damage. Glass also prevents the painting from being fully present. You just can't *see* a painting under glass.

I don't care what anybody says: The nonreflective glass is even worse; it absolutely embalms paintings. But even under ordinary glass, the texture is blunted, there are all those damned reflections of ugly light fixtures in the gallery or other people or yourself, and the art just doesn't breathe. No painter I can think of ever intended his paintings to be viewed through a sheet of glass mounted a quarter inch above the paint surface. In most museums, the lighting is so terrible that looking at paintings under glass isn't much different from looking at reproductions. If anything, it's worse.

The public doesn't know any better. The public, for the most part, probably hasn't noticed the way glass has become ubiquitous. The public glances at the art and then stampedes to the gift shop anyway. Well, what can I say? It's the same public that has come to accept sex with condoms. The principles are quite similar. We live in an age of risk, where it is no longer safe for a painting in a public collection to be regarded with the naked eye.

I set her free of that hateful glass, and then, before I

put the panel back into its frame—an excellent Dutch frame, probably eighteenth century, very severe black wood, it's precisely the right frame for the painting, not one of those "I am a masterpiece" ornate gilt plaster job-bies in which some museums mistakenly imprison their seventeenth-century Dutch pictures—I just sat with the simple painted panel in my two hands and I looked and I looked and I looked. And anything that might happen to me when this is over, however it ends, will be worth that hour.

And no, I don't know precisely how they did it, though I'm not naïve.

I hope no one was hurt.

I didn't ask.

29th of January, cold and clear

―――――

MICKEY AND I stayed up all that night talking. I did not go into this blindly. He was right: The conversation did change my life.

Mickey volunteered for the Provos when he was fifteen. It was something he says he always knew he would do, from the time he was a little boy. The Troubles, as they are called here—a simple term for a complex situation—were part of daily life, despite the tranquillity of West Cork. Every evening after the milking, his father would go up the road to the only pub with a television set, where he would gather with some of the men in the village to watch the news of the day's bombings and shootings in the North and drink pints and talk politics.

By age five, Mickey would accompany his father and

sit on the bar, building houses with beer mats, eating packets of crisps, listening and watching and taking it all in. He was nourished on that hatred, on those obsessions with secrets and retribution.

To sign up with the IRA, Mickey traveled to the North from Dublin, where he told his family he'd gone to spend the weekend with a friend he met at Gaeltacht in Donegal, the traditional summer school to which lots of Irish kids are sent to study Irish. (Based on Mickey's reports, fluency and romance seem to develop in equal measure in those summer interludes.)

His friend Eamonn O'Doherty was a handsome lad from Howth who had an easy way with all the girls and made people laugh with his brilliant imitations of the priests and nuns who taught them their classes. Mickey, who says he himself was a "pimply, stupid git," looked up to him tremendously.

Eamonn recruited Mickey into his section, which was made up of lads just like Mickey—passionate boys, raw patriots eager to give up their lives for a free and united Ireland, and eager for weapons more sophisticated than "beggars' bullets"—rocks.

"It's a wonder I wasn't killed three or four times over" is about all Mickey said about his first months as a volunteer, before changing the subject. That's the extent of what he has told me, but I gather he was used as a donkey to carry bomb-making equipment and to plant bombs, and I'm fairly certain he had a hand in assembling them, as well.

The reason I think so is because when we were at Pete's, Mickey was strangely horrified when I offered him and Pete some traditional Christmas fruitcake, the kind that's roofed with a marzipan slab of icing. It was late, and they were well into the Red Breast, which might account for Mickey's unguarded reaction. He pushed away the plate, muttering that he loathes marzipan because it smells so much like gelignite, which, he added, gives him terrible headaches.

His innocent face has always helped him to travel freely. Apparently, although he's been active for ten years now, he's never been arrested and might not even be on the list of known IRA activists.

There is one more thing Mickey told me about those years: His friend Eamonn was killed beside him as they ran away from a Bogside volunteer action of some kind, probably a bombing organized by their Derry brigade. A British sniper got him. They were both seventeen years old.

We didn't have much time.

We had ten days before the show closed in The Hague, perhaps another two or three before the paintings would start to leave Holland. Because it was the final venue, the show would no longer travel as one shipment, but instead, piecemeal, each painting would be returning to its home at the convenience of the lending institution. This would make our work simpler, with the right preparation.

Starting that night and continuing into the days ahead, Mickey asked me a lot of very specific questions and I answered them to the best of my ability. Whenever I would say I didn't know, he would persuade me to apply my imagination and my logical mind, and soon enough I would give him some kind of answer.

All business now, he would conduct a flurry of calls each night on a secure cell phone after rounds of questions and answers. The painting was called "Betty's package" whenever it was referred to. Mickey would listen, relay more questions to me, and repeat my answers in carefully coded language that didn't ever sound as if it carried any meaning at all. Several times he muttered, "Ring me back in ten," and worked with me against the ticking clock. The phone always rang precisely ten minutes later, and by then I would have prepared some answers, and they—whoever they were, wherever they were—the others—would have come up with more questions.

A couple of times, Mickey went into my bathroom, locked the door, and ran the faucets in the tub full force in order to have some sort of private chat. I couldn't afford to let it bother me. This was how it worked; this is how these things are done.

I provided him with a huge volume of information, from phrases people in the museum world use to descriptions of how a courier manages the paperwork and logistics at the airport and what the shipping invoices look like, and how the insurance company sets guidelines for security precautions.

At work—unbelievably, I was still going in to work at the library during these days, keeping to my normal schedule—I was very discreetly able to access some correspondence files on various computer links we share with museums that were exhibition lenders, and I found out a great deal of specific information about precise arrangements after the show's closing.

A casual conversation with the right curator produced the name of the staffer at the National Gallery in London who had landed the return courier assignment for the queen's Vermeer, which would travel with the paintings lent by the National Gallery in London.

The Frick curator who supplied me with this nugget, Fred Lewis, a myopic little man with a huge handlebar mustache, which I think he must groom every morning, like a pet, also volunteered that he'd kept an eye on me with my Irish cousin, to whom I'd introduced him when we were walking together through the underground passage that connects the library building with the Frick mansion. I always feel as if I'm on a secret cultural mission when I'm in that tunnel—it's part of the whole elegant, hidden, rarefied feel of the Frick.

Fred told me that when we'd been through the galleries that first afternoon he kept noticing Mickey looking around, and he kept thinking about the Irish Vermeer having been stolen from Russborough House in Dublin on two different occasions in the last twenty-five years. Both thefts, he reminded me, had been organized by the IRA. *Lady Writing a Letter with Her Maid* was only recovered in Brussels in 1993. I had seen it for the first time in Washington.

"Faith and begorra, 'tis a close watch they'll be keepin' on that wee precious canvas on its way back to Dublin." Fred smirked, using an outrageous lucky leprechaun accent. "In case the IRA is hopin' the third time's the charm."

Oblivious to my frozen response, he added, "Do you know why they had the famine? The poor Paddys planted the potatoes, but then they couldn't find them!"

Ha ha.

So I was in. There was never a precise moment when I agreed to participate, now that I think about it. Nor was there a moment when I said, No, stop, I'm not doing this; don't ask me to do this.

It seemed so right, so inevitable. Do I keep saying that, protesting too much? That's really how it felt. Only when I was searching the computer files for information to help Mickey did I realize that I had agreed, that I was, in fact, taking part in a conspiracy to break the law, to steal.

I imagined myself in the eyes of my colleagues at the library—an efficient, rather cold, humorless person, a woman on her own, someone neither adventurous nor passionate. It was exciting to sit there among them, going through my usual routine, knowing that, like Mickey, I was beyond suspicion. It was during that conversation with Fred Lewis, when I felt the force of his casual contempt for the Irish in a new and personal way, that I realized what utter certainty I felt about the rightness of my participation.

I know that Mickey used my passion for Vermeer, that he knew perfectly well about my expertise from his intelligence sources, whatever they are. It's one of the many things about which I have no knowledge whatsoever, and no need to know, though I have to admit I'm both flattered and apprehensive that Mickey was virtually sent to find me in order to assess the possibilities of a successful plan to do this, to take a Vermeer and ransom it for 10 million pounds sterling. He used my passion in all ways. And I let him.

I made my best guesses about painting crates and shipping protocols and hundreds of other details. Presumably, most of my information was useful. Which makes me an accessory from the outset, I know. I will say this again, because I want to be clear about it: I have gone every step of the way of my own free will and with my eyes open.

Mickey was very taken with my inspired invention of a double-sided crate with a hidden compartment, something I finally sketched out for him after much talk. "How would you switch a fake for a real painting?" he kept asking. "What would be the right moment?"

When I was a child, Paddy gave me a little balsa-wood box, a magic trick that made nickels disappear or turn into dimes, which worked on the same principles. My idea was to supply a supposedly empty crate that would have a hidden fake loaded in, so that whenever the real painting was removed, the false back would go with it and the fake would be put into place. That way, inventory counts would never be off for even a moment, though for a time the crate would actually contain *two* paintings. Someone would have to get a very good look at the empty crates in storage, so that the new crate would be a perfect match for the original crate. The fake crate would require more counterfeiting skill than would the fake painting.

The most important thing about the fake painting, I emphasized, was that the frame had to be a perfect match, because once those pictures were unbolted from the walls at the Mauritshuis, they were each going to be placed, ever so carefully, into their custom-made felt-lined numbered crates, one by one, with all sorts of checklists and security sign-offs, and once the side runners were screwed into place over the slotted tracks, nobody was going to want the hassle, or the responsibility, of taking them off again, just so long as there was no reason to check, so long as nothing out of the ordinary attracted anybody's attention.

And—I love this—given that a painting under glass is hard to scrutinize at an angle, a pretty ordinary fake would suffice; a cheap reproduction would do it. Such as the ones for sale in museum gift shops everywhere Vermeers are hanging on museum walls. We have them at the Frick, they were in the National Gallery, and I was sure they were for sale at the Mauritshuis. Most of the smaller paintings are reproduced full size, on a canvaslike textured board. People buy them. The Frick gift shop sells a couple of hundred a year. For about twenty dollars, you can buy a "deluxe" version of *The Music Lesson*, on a stressed-wood panel that really does look pretty authentic. It's the most popular Vermeer reproduction in the shop, perhaps because it's so small—about the size of a sandwich.

The new crate with its hidden duplicate was to be switched at the Mauritshuis as soon as possible, while the show was still hanging. So by the time they took the show down, it would be there, ready for the Mauritshuis staff to place *The Music Lesson* into its custom-built slot.

With the exhibition still on the walls, though, security around the empty packing crates wasn't likely to be too intense. And the crate for *The Music Lesson* would be one of the smallest, probably only about twenty-four inches square, relatively easy to conceal.

Smuggling the new crate for *The Music Lesson* in would be no problem, I was told. We had someone in and out of there all the time right now, a sleeper on the maintenance staff; his diagrams of the building had been on hand for more than a year. But removing the old crate might be awkward. It would have to be destroyed or altered inside the building, Mickey fretted, or its premature discovery could tip the whole thing.

I solved that stumbling block very simply—some huge FRAGILE stickers to slap over the Queen's Gallery/Buckingham Palace identifications, a prepared stencil, a small jar of odorless quick-drying paint, and a stencil brush would do the trick. In a matter of seconds, the crate could be given a different identification, say, the Städelsches Kunstinstitut, Frankfurt-am-Main, and don't forget the umlaut. Then mark the crate EMPTY (and find out the Dutch and German words for *empty*, and write it in Dutch and German as well as in English) and 1974 or something equally meaningless and misleading with a blue grease pencil in several places, and then shift the crate to the very back of a storage area. I know what museum storage areas are like, and even though the

Dutch are tidy, my guess is that crate won't be examined for many years.

The actual *Music Lesson* is so small—not quite six by seven inches. If the removal of the genuine painting was to go undetected, with the decoy painting in place, there is no reason to think that the switch would be discovered for a very long while. The most important thing, I realized, was to pinpoint the weakest security moment, when the crate could be approached with the least amount of observation. That, I suggested, would probably be at the airport, after the careful Dutch had signed off, and not before.

Apparently, my suggestions were useful.

Part of the understanding has been, from that first night, that I would not ask any questions at all. In the beginning, whenever I did blurt out an irresistible question, Mickey would go silent, simply not answer, which I hated, and it taught me to stop soon enough. What I don't know can't hurt me, and what I don't know can't hurt anyone else.

They succeeded. I believe the painting was removed at Schiphol Airport, in the British Airways freight area, though I don't know the precise circumstances. I don't know if there was a violent confrontation of any kind, or if it was all done surreptitiously. I do know that it had been established from the outset that any guards who were in the wrong place at the wrong time would be handcuffed to radiators or pipes and duct tape would be used to blindfold them as well as to bind them, so even though they would suspect that something had been stolen, they would have a hard time figuring out exactly what, and the ensuing confusion would buy valuable time. But my sense of the actuality of any of this is based only on movies and television. I have no idea how they pulled it off, and I don't want to know. I prefer to imagine that it was clever and clean.

I don't know, for instance, when the theft was detected, though it's highly likely that the discovery wasn't made before the picture was uncrated in London. Then there would have been some confusion about where the actual crime took place, and under whose jurisdiction. Perhaps for those reasons, perhaps because of the ransom—I'm not really sure quite why—the theft hasn't been made public even now.

Mickey told me it "went off a bomb," which terrified me at first, until we sorted out our linguistic differences. I was, as per instruction, in the call box next to Nolan's pub, in the middle of Ballyroe, across from O'Mahoney's, and Mickey was who knows where. The connection was bad and it was a very brief call, and as it was the first time I had heard Mickey's voice since New York, I was desperate to keep hearing it. Kieran O'Mahoney was watching me from his shop. Annie Dunne was watching me from hers. I turned my back, spooked by a silly sense that they could somehow discern the content of the call by the look on my face.

Mickey meant that it had gone off brilliantly. I didn't believe him at first, especially since there had been nothing at all in the newspapers or on BBC radio.

Waiting, alone in the cottage day after day all through that interminable week, I had gone from my moments of exalted wonderment at my body, my mind, the beauty of the universe, et cetera, to paranoic fantasies that this was in fact an elaborate practical joke or hoax of which I was the butt. Or was I being victimized in some other way? Was my apartment being ransacked at this moment? Was Mickey after my money? Had I been taken in by some sort of weird con? Then, when a mental review of every aspect persuaded me that it was real, I wondered for a little while if I was the pawn in a dangerous political game I didn't understand at all.

It was hard to believe, because, I confess, the whole scheme had really seemed like a lark to me, like some elaborate role-playing fantasy, a wonderful game, a game in which I was thrilled to be invited to participate. Even as I organized my indefinite leave of absence from the library, packed up some clothing, organized some bills that needed paying, telephoned Pete with a vague explanation about visiting Ireland with Mickey, bought my ticket, and got on that plane (Mickey having unexpectedly disappeared two days before, leaving me a muttered one-sentence message on my machine saying he'd see me "at home"), right through to my arrival at the cottage in Gortbreac Cove as per detailed instructions, it all seemed like a tremendously exciting adventure, a crazy fantasy.

And I hadn't actually had any IRA contact, other than with Mickey, I mean, until I began to get his messages. So nothing about any of my activities matched my notion of what IRA operations are like. (Which notion was, I think, something highly cinematic involving Harrison Ford in pursuit of sinister men in black balaclavas.) I had yet to see a gun. I have yet to see a gun.

But they had done it. I didn't know it, but they had done it on the third day I was in Ballyroe. I was worried that the scheme had failed because I had heard nothing. I was getting antsy, and every day that passed, when I had convinced myself all over again that this insane plan was in fact real, I was worried that something had gone horribly wrong.

It had occurred to me midweek that I had no way to get in touch with Mickey, and having never had any contact with anyone else, I was completely on my own. I worried that he had been injured. I realized that I had no idea if Mickey was supposed to participate in the actual operation in The Hague. If not, then where was he? In some underground Belfast IRA headquarters? Just up the road in Rosscarbery? I began to get angry. I went for little walks and shivered in the cold and drank too many pots of tea and listened to the BBC on the radio every hour and I tried not to let myself panic that I was simply abandoned here in Ballyroe and would never hear from him again.

Mickey's people had not anticipated that the Dutch police and Interpol and Downing Street and MI5—whoever the consortium of intergalactic security people is for a case involving a mega art theft of the queen's property—would keep the theft under wraps. I had no way to know it, but by the time the painting was in Ballyroe, the ransom demand for 10 million pounds in the form of untraceable gold bullion had already been phoned to Buckingham Palace.

Where had the painting been in those eight days between the time it was taken and the time it came to me? Mickey made a passing remark shortly before he vanished from New York about how those houseboats on the Amstel are surprisingly comfortable, which makes me think that it might have been transported to Amsterdam from The Hague, but that might not be the case, either. The great information specialist might also be a disinformation specialist, it occurs to me.

It's astonishing to look at this painting and not know where it has been, to know that it has traveled through city streets, on highways, and that it has passed through the world—a world that claims to care very much about this painting—but the world had no knowledge that it was there. Is *The Music Lesson* still beautiful when it is wrapped in bubble wrap in a Samsonite suitcase?

At the beginning of artistic production, Walter Benjamin writes, there were ceremonial objects: "What mattered was their existence, not their being on view." He goes on to say, "Today, the cult value would seem to demand that the work of art remain hidden...the work of art in prehistoric times...by the absolute emphasis on its cult value...was, first and foremost, an instrument of magic."

The Music Lesson is an instrument of magic. Perhaps now it is also an instrument of change, a talisman, the charm that will force powerful people to pay attention and take decisive action at last.

Those involved in transporting the painting probably would have no particular personal reaction to it. Would they stop to look at it for a moment in a museum? It might not be beautiful to them. Its beauty might lie in its purported worth, or in its provenance. Or maybe its beauty would be in its symbolic value in the eyes of those men who possibly risked their lives to move the briefcase, or the box, or the duffel, or whatever protective shipping material the painting has traveled in all this way.

The little elderly man who brought the painting to

me, for instance, probably had no clue that he was transporting a priceless seventeenth-century painting in the back of his delivery van, property of HRH. But I don't know if he was an operative or really just a deliveryman. He arrived in the middle of the afternoon, when as many people as possible could see him. He got lost and stopped along the way for directions to Gortbreac Cove. Twice. He played his part a little more thoroughly than he needed to, in fact, standing around looking hopeful until I gave him two pounds for his efforts.

My delivery didn't look anything like a priceless work of art. It looked like an ordinary gray Samsonite suitcase. Said suitcase, I was careful to mention to Kieran O'Mahoney with calculated dudgeon the following morning, had finally been found by Aer Lingus after all these days missing. Can you believe the airline would pay that fellow fifty pounds just to bring it out to me? It's a wonder they can keep the planes in the air, et cetera.

I suppose whoever flew it into Cork might have thought it was a cache of weapons, or drugs. I will probably never know very much about how it all worked. I don't really care. The painting is here, and for these days, it's mine. It's my instrument of magic and it has brought Mickey to me and it will bring change for the people of Ireland.

Queen Elizabeth I was so much more interesting than the present queen, whom Mickey mockingly calls

Betty Windsor and nothing else. Though I suppose when I think of the first Elizabeth, I'm really thinking of Glenda Jackson, whom I admire. More people have probably seen Glenda Jackson playing the queen in those *Masterpiece Theatre* productions than ever actually saw the genuine article. Which is more real, then, to us? Whom do we mean when we say Queen Elizabeth?

I wonder if the queen misses her painting. I wonder if she knows it's gone, or if she's been kept in the dark. I wonder if she cares about her paintings, about this painting. After all, it hasn't got dogs in it. I wonder, quite seriously, if B. W. has ever really *looked* at this painting. But maybe the woman deserves more credit than that. If I try, maybe I can imagine her having long, fascinating conversations about it with, oh, I don't know, Anthony Blunt, before he died. Before he was exposed.

His art writing is quite wonderful, but now, when I read him, I cannot help but consider the context of his having been a Soviet spy all those years. Does it change the way he looked at art? Perhaps not. Does it change the way we read Anthony Blunt? How can it not?

The queen's face is on millions of coins and millions of stamps. She is reproduced, represented as a work of art, like a classical Greek or Roman head. And yet, this face before me on a tiny painting, this private face with its bemused smile that isn't quite a smile, this woman with her glorious quality of actualness on the verge of creating music—she is largely unknown, not imprinted on the average mind in that iconographic sense, not as real.

Perhaps if I were a Brit, I would feel differently about this, but I don't believe the queen deserves to own *The Music Lesson*. How could she?

Queen Elizabeth I hated the Dutch, calling them "swag-bellied Dutch butter-boxes." King James I probably hated them, too—his consort, Anne of Denmark, was said by the first Earl of Salisbury to prefer the company of her paintings to living people. But by the seventeenth century, King Charles I and other royals quite liked to sit for portraits by Dutch painters. And of course, let's not forget the Dutch king of England, William III, aka William of Orange, who was born in The Hague and painted by Van Dyck (the House of Orange still reigns in the Netherlands); who really began the Troubles in 1690 with his victory over his Catholic father-in-law, poor old King James II, at the Battle of the Boyne.

It's really perfect, when you think of it, that to commemorate the battle, the Brits named a flower sweet William, while the Irish christened a weed stinking Billy.

When George III bought *The Music Lesson* in 1762 as part of a large collection of Dutch paintings, it was attributed to Frans van Mieris. Which is to say that Vermeer came into the royal collection by accident. And there it was scorned, too, until this century. A nineteenth-century guide to the royal collection—a copy is in the Frick Art Reference Library—described this sublime little painting as "very awkward and tasteless, the figure being too far back."

Oh, those entitled Brits. Even when they do not value what is good and precious they trample and possess. Not this time. No number of Orangemen marching in their silly sashes every twelfth of July will ever change what the Irish know and feel. And the victory of *The Music Lesson* will be ours.

3lst of January, blustery, raw, clear

TWO DAYS LATER. Something happened this morning that shouldn't have happened.

I had been reading since waking quite early, long
before the sun rose (which in these short, dark months,
it doesn't do until well after eight o'clock), and now was
making toast for a late breakfast, which in the kitchen of
the cottage is a complicated process that's essentially like
broiling something. Sometimes I feel as if I'm cooking
over a campfire. I don't mind it, but it takes concentra-
tion. The bread has to be turned, and then the second
side goes very quickly, especially if it's a thick slice of
Irish brown cake.

I was reading *The Book of Evidence* by John Banville,
which I had picked up at the Dublin Airport the morn-

ing I landed. It's a novel a colleague of mine at the Frick had told me about, and I had been meaning to read it anyway. But having read about two-thirds of it last night and this morning, I had become quite unsettled, before Mary came to the door. *The Book of Evidence* is about a man who has committed a brutal murder in the course of stealing a painting—a Dutch portrait that sounds like a Rembrandt, though it might also be a Hals—with which he is obsessed. It feels like a personal message to me, and it makes me apprehensive.

Mary Carew hallooed me as I was messing around in the kitchen. I had the front door ajar because it was a relatively soft day with a little bit of watery sunlight, and the broiler was a bit smoky because of burning fat that must have splashed out of the pan last night when I roasted the most intensely perfect, brilliantly flavored free-range chicken of my entire life.

I must add here that I had been studying *The Music Lesson* in the early-morning light, and had not put it back into the Samsonite suitcase. I know this doesn't make sense, but sometimes I have a compulsion to let her have space and air, as if she could breathe, as if a painting could feel, could have claustrophobia. (I've taken the glass out of the frame every time I look at the painting, too.) Which is to say I had left the painting out, leaning against the back of a chair in the upstairs middle room.

"Patricia, good morning to you. Are you receiving?

I've just brought you some warm scones and a little pot of
my bramble jelly," Mary called out as she put her head
around the door. "They're your brambles from September
last, actually, or poor old Denny's, God rest his soul. The
sweetest brambles in Gortbreac grow right here beside
your door, you know. Denny was mad for my bramble
jelly. He had a sweet tooth, the old todger." As she came
in, she knocked on the door frame with a woolly-gloved
knuckle, this formality retroactively legitimizing her
intrusion.

I reflexively invited Mary in—I had to, as she was
already well inside the door, peering around the place,
her admission ticket the knotted plastic carrier bag from
O'Mahoney's shop containing the scones and jam jar
that was now outstretched in my direction. I took it from
her and thanked her and set the things on the counter
and asked her if she would like a cup of tea, and she said
she wouldn't mind, which is a yes, I have learned from
experience with Mickey.

Mary removed her ancient waxed jacket, a long, agri-
culturally aromatic green farmer's coat that probably
once belonged to her dead husband, and hung it on a
hook located behind the door, which told me that she
has visited here in the cottage on other occasions. She
sat down at the table, looking around carefully, while I
made sure to scald the pot and measure in the loose tea
and pour the water from the whistling kettle after resting

when it goes off the boil, just as I have also learned from Mickey. Mary commented on how unusual it is for a Yank to know how to make a proper cup of tea, and I told her I had an Irish grandfather who taught me (which is actually untrue—Paddy wasn't much of a tea drinker), and that's when the toast caught fire.

When smoke fills a kitchen, inevitably, by the time you react, there's a sense of déjà vu—the smoke you see, you have already seen, but you haven't noticed it until you do. Now there was gray smoke hanging in the air, thickening by the moment like a sudden fog. I wrapped my hand in a threadbare dish towel and snatched the broiler rack from the oven. There were flames, and heavier smoke billowed out the open oven door. In a matter of seconds, I was able to cross the few steps to the door and fling the wire rack onto the ground outside, where the two flaming chips of charcoal that had been my toast burnt out to embers in a matter of moments.

"Och, Patricia, praise God you've got young reflexes," Mary breathed behind me, fanning the air with *The Book of Evidence*, which had been tented on the counter where I like to have my morning tea and toast. I know it's odd, but if I'm reading something that's really exciting—or upsetting—sometimes I read standing up.

"But look, you've burnt your pretty hand."

My left hand had a wide red mark across the palm,

like a branded life line, where the edge of the broiling pan had burned me through the thin weave of the dish towel. As I looked at it dumbly, it began to hurt.

"You'll want cold water on that, let's put your hand under the tap straight away," Mary said, taking me by the elbow and leading me over to the kitchen sink.

I stood at the sink for a few minutes while the cold water gushed over my hand. Mary asked if I had any "plasters," about, and I didn't know what she meant. I thought she was proposing to apply some quaint sort of poultice, or a homemade cast. I asked her about that, and she didn't answer. I thought she was still standing directly behind me—over the rushing sound of the tap water, I didn't hear her going up the stairs.

"Is a plaster something you do with bandages?" I repeated. I turned around then, shutting off the water. She wasn't there. The floorboards creaked overhead. Then I could hear her steps on the stairs, coming back down.

"You should always keep plasters about, Patricia," Mary admonished as she stepped carefully off the steepish bottom step onto the uneven concrete floor. "Look, I've taken an old pillow slip that shan't be missed out of the hall cupboard. We can use strips of this to cover the burn until you get some plasters at O'Mahoney's. And some good ointment to keep away infection. That's important. Och, it's swelling a bit. Does it pain you, love?"

My heart began to pound. I tried to stammer out a reply. My hand really did hurt, but I was paralyzed by my fear that she had seen the painting. I tried to envision her route upstairs. If she had turned to the right and gone directly to the cupboard outside my bedroom where she found the pillowcase—pillow slip—then she might have seen nothing. But Mary is a snoop, and, like most of the village, she's curious about Denis's cottage since the improvements. And it's very small; only a few steps in any direction and you've seen it all.

"Patricia, you're looking pale. You should sit down. Do you feel faint?" she asked me sharply. We sat down together on the two hard wooden seats (Nora calls them "fool's chairs") by the cold fireplace in the sitting room. My fires keep going out. I don't have the hang of banking the coals at night, though Nora has tried to show me how twice. A downdraft stirred the ashes.

"I think I'm okay, Mary." I tried to sound like my normal self, whatever that sounds like. My words sounded false, like a lie. "Really. I'm fine." She was tearing the pillow slip into long, limp white strips in her lap, and when she was done, she wrapped my hand carefully until it was neatly bound. She tied the ends of the bandage with a neat flourish, murmuring, "Matthew Walker should hold it for a while."

"Who?"

"Och, Matthew Walker. It's the name of a knot. One of George's favorite sailing knots. 'Tis what you call it when you make the knot from the strands at the end of the one rope, love. I used it a great deal for bandages during the war. I drove an ambulance, you know. Had to be handy with the bandages."

This was momentarily surprising, though, on reflection, I guess it's not particularly amazing, given her age. Ireland, was, of course, neutral (it would have been impossible to side with the Brits), but Mary wasn't living here then.

"Were you at the front?"

"Och, no, I didn't go to war at all; the war came to me. I was in London during the Blitz. Praise God those days are past. Though it's still possible to get blown to bits if you're in the wrong place at the wrong time, I suppose. I'd rather take a coach tour to one of those Arab countries where they're always squabbling amongst themselves than set foot in Harrods, I'll tell you that." She gave a little shake to her head, like a dog distracted by a fly. She looked troubled. I still didn't know where I was with her, what she had seen during her upstairs tour.

"Now, love, how's the hand?"

"Well, I'm sure Matthew Walker will see me into the village later, and I will get some antibiotic ointment and some plasters. It hurts. But I'm okay, really. No big deal."

Mary started to say something and stopped. I realized that I didn't want to hear her speak about the painting—I was afraid to hear her say anything about it—and I rushed to speak instead, to keep her from saying she had seen it.

"Thank you, Mary. Really. I appreciate your binding up my wound and all. I feel ridiculous, burning the toast. And now your tea's cold." I was flustered, hoping still that I had been lucky, that this was merely a close call.

"'Band-Aids'? Isn't that what you Yanks call them?" Mary gave it an absurd attempt at an American inflection. We laughed together, and Mary went into the kitchen to put the kettle on for a fresh pot of tea, insisting that I stay in my chair by the dead fire. It made me think of Mickey, and all the little moments between us in those New York days when our conversations had constantly smacked into hair slides or barrettes, face flannels or washcloths, kerbs or sidewalks, strands or beaches, queues or lines.

When one night, in bed, Mickey had reached up and lifted the hair out of my eyes and told me I ought to cut my hair in a fringe, I had laughed, envisioning something on a Victorian lamp shade. But a moment later, "bangs" had made him laugh, as he said, "like a drain," until he was out of breath, and I couldn't really defend the logic of such a term.

Thinking of Mickey made me miss him, but then I was fearful again. He would be angry if she had glimpsed the painting. I don't think he has ever been angry at me. I don't know what he would do. What would he do? What had she seen?

"It's a lovely little thing you've got up there, Patricia," Mary said quietly, standing in the doorway to the sitting room, wiping out a tea mug with the singed dish towel. She spoke so softly, it almost registered as a thought inside my head rather than spoken words. "You know, I was presented at court when I was eighteen," she continued in a low voice, as if she was telling me a soothing bedtime story. "My uncle, my mother's brother, he was Lord Samuel Swift, chancellor of the Exchequer. You've never heard of him, I'm sure. I'll never forget that day. The finery everywhere. The uniforms on the guards. It was grand. The tea in the tiniest, thinnest cups you can imagine, like flower petals. The paintings on the walls."

I stared at her. She stared back. She looked…disappointed. I didn't know what to say. I can't imagine who she thought I was right then, what she thought I was thinking. What was I thinking? That I had ruined something important. That my carelessness had put everything at risk.

I started to stammer out some reply, some reasonable account, an impossible explanation that would undo her impression and shape it another way, and Mary interrupted me, looking down at her feet, avoiding my eyes.

"Don't," she said sharply. "You owe me no explanations. 'Tis none of my business what you've got up in that room or how it got there. If I've learned anything at all, living in this corner of this country all these years, it's to keep my mouth shut. Tell me nothing and I'll know nothing."

She went back into the kitchen and I could hear the sounds of her tea making, and then she returned with a brimming mug that she gently put into my right hand.

"I've given you just a drop of milk. Do drink it while it's hot, Patricia; it'll calm you." She wouldn't look at me; she was speaking with her gaze averted again. "I hope you'll see to that burn. Will you, love? Let me know if you need anything. I'll be on my way, now, if you don't mind. No, no, don't get up."

She got her coat and let herself out the door.

I went for a walk. I didn't know what else to do, and I really did need those plasters, or something for my burn, so I wrapped up the painting and put it away in the suitcase inside the cupboard and locked everything up carefully, and then I walked down into the village. The sunlight was pale, lemony, too bright for the day, somehow. I met Nora with some of her cows on the road, and I put my hand into my pocket so as to avoid a conversation about it.

"One of those false spring days," she warned, wacking the muddy back end of a cow with a stick for no apparent reason. "Pay it no mind. There'll be a gale before the end of the week. And we've got the AI man scheduled for Friday."

I didn't know who the AI man was, and she explained that it was an artificial-insemination service for her cows.

"Isn't calving in the spring?" My hand throbbed. I was sorry I had asked a question and now had to listen to the answer.

"That's nature's way, but not the AI way—Hugh O'Keeffe's got new twin calves just born Sunday week. You can calve all the year round now. 'Tis more efficient to space them out. Some here, some there, instead of all at once. No mucking around with a bull. It's all modern. If 'twas up to the women, half the country would have their kiddies the same way, no more mucking around."

On the walk back, with a tube of antibiotic ointment possibly intended for livestock and a packet of plasters, I tried to sort my thoughts. I had a headache. I wished I had bought aspirin. What did I feel? I didn't know. It's so hard for me to know what I feel under ordinary circumstances, and I was just flooded with fear, and guilt. How could I have been so careless?

Mr. O'Mahoney in the shop had been curious about my hand and about my purchases, but he hadn't asked directly, and I had deflected all of his usual opening gambits with shrugs and distracted monosyllabic replies. Pete calls that "taking the conversational ball and putting it in your pocket."

I was unusually fatigued by the long walk down and back. I had a profound desire to crawl back into bed and take a nap. Daylight was almost at an end, by now clouds had massed together into a leaden sky, imperceptibly, and I was cold. There was a chilly breeze that hadn't been anywhere about when I left the cottage, or I would have worn a heavier jacket over my sweater. Everything was gray. It was a relief when I was in sight of the cottage once again.

I had trouble with the key at the door—the lock seemed wrong—and as I tried to turn the key again, the knob turned and the door opened from the inside.

Someone was there.

I was terrified.

Then I heard Mickey's laugh.

When he put his arms around me, I started to cry. I was so relieved that he was there, and at the same time I suddenly felt how alone I had been up until that moment.

"So, how're ye keeping?" Mickey asked mockingly, holding me at arm's length for a moment, looking me up and down. "You've almost gone native," he said, taking in my not particularly clean hair and my mud-caked boots and the various wool- and flannel-covered parts in-between.

We held each other for a long time without speaking, just standing there, totally still. It was hard to believe he was here—paradoxically, he seemed too large, the wrong scale, out of place here in the front room of the cottage, just a few miles from his own village. He appeared tired, worn-out. Older. I touched his face and he took my hand in his and gazed at me intently. *So this is what it is to be known.*

"The roasty chicken was really brilliant. I finished it. Hope you don't mind," Mickey muttered into my hair a moment later, hugging me again. "I hadn't eaten a proper meal in a couple of days. I haven't slept very much, either."

"Oh, Mix, I'll cook proper meals for you. Where have you been? What have you been doing? What's going on?"

Silence.

"Oh shit, Mickey," I said crossly, pushing myself out of his embrace. We were still out of sync after the separation, not quite connecting. "Fine, don't tell me where you've been. Don't tell me what's going on. Obviously, I can't be trusted."

"Patricia."

"What?"

"I'm sorry. I've been the last three nights in a filthy shed about four miles from here, and I haven't been particularly comfortable, and I've got a lot on my mind."

I hugged him again, feeling guilty for my relative comforts and privileges—and lack of responsibilities—and for putting him on the spot.

"But please don't pressure me, Patricia. We're both a little tense."

"Paddy used to say he was as jumpy as a long-tailed cat in a room full of rocking chairs when he was out of sorts."

Mickey snorted and pulled me close to him. Sparring with him this way, seeing him so unexpectedly, I suddenly wanted him very badly. We kissed, briefly, then again, more seriously, searchingly. "I missed that warm cunny of yours," he whispered, melting me. I slid my hands up inside his shirt and then began to rummage in his pants. Mickey's hands ranged over my shirts and sweaters and leggings and jeans with increasing urgency until he broke away from our kissing to exclaim, "Good Christ, Patricia, I can't find you at all under your horse blankets."

We went up to bed then, unbuttoning as we climbed the stairs.

I've woken after the deepest of sleeps. It's night, and the steady drum of rain might be what woke me. And I was hungry. My bare shoulders were cold, too. I covered Mickey, who seemed just now to be sleeping twenty thousand leagues under the sea, that near-coma sleep of the exhausted. I'm downstairs at the table, drinking tea and eating a boiled egg and most of the scones Mary brought—I never did have supper—and trying to think clearly.

I don't know what sort of future I really see with Mickey. I don't know what we have. It's a powerful connection, but it might not have a place in the real world. I know that. But in the past few hours, we have been together in a world of our own, where words don't count, where there are no politics, where there is nothing but all the simplicity and all the glory of that very basic joining together. We don't know each other very well, but in those moments, we know each other deeply, and if I don't know the small truths of every detail of these weeks, I do know the larger and profound truth of the way my body and my mind have truly been met by Mickey's body and mind. When we meet, it is a rare and perfect thing.

In the morning, I know, I will have to tell Mickey about Mary seeing the painting. My time alone has consisted of a series of simple moments. Every simple moment has become more complicated in an instant with Mickey here. This account book, for instance, isn't something I want him to find, and so I'll have to sneak around, which I don't like. I'm relieved that he's here at last, but I think I miss my solitude.

I sat for about an hour with the painting just now. It's getting late. I was thinking about what it is in Dutch interiors that has always drawn me, since childhood: the quality of safety, the sense of resolution, an exactness, a specificity, a devotion to order, a celebration of dailiness. What Cartier-Bresson called the decision in every moment. There is a sense that a painting can contain knowledge, information, beautiful information. And Vermeer was never only about content. He wanted to capture what's visible—tones, not the simulation but the situation of a tapestry on a table. He painted the blur, the wedge of light at the edge of what we are looking at, not just the thing we are looking at. He painted the way we see, not just what we see.

I have always wanted to live in those rooms. Here, on this wild coast, I have lived in those rooms. So much of my time has been squandered on an approximation of a life, a description of a life. But in these days here, I have been truly present, truly alive.

When I worked on my thesis, I discovered a wonderful remark by Henry James about his travels in Holland: "When you are looking at the originals, you seem to be looking at the copies; and when you are looking at the copies, you seem to be looking at the originals. Is it a canal-side in Haarlem, or is it a Van der Heyden?... The maid-servants in the streets seem to have stepped out of the frame of a Gerald Dow and appear equally well-adapted for stepping back again."

I will never know this woman—I will never know

her name, or the music she is about to play. I don't know what foods she likes, or if she has children. She remains silent. But I have come to know what she represents very well. And I am grateful for her lesson, for what she has taught me about integrity, and constancy. Through her, I have come to know myself, and I have begun to understand the world a little better, too. I have to figure out ways to live in my own rooms. I have started to recognize my strengths as well as my weaknesses. Some of my strengths, it turns out, *were* my weaknesses.

I don't know how much longer I will have her to myself. Mickey's presence makes me think that possibly this was the last time I will have had the privilege and luxury of this singular communion. It will be a sad moment when I have to give her up. Life seems sometimes like nothing more than a series of losses, from beginning to end. That's the given. How you respond to those losses, what you make of what's left, that's the part you have to make up as you go.

1st of February, very dark

———

MARY CAREW was found dead this morning, in her chicken house, lying in the chicken litter with her head next to a pan of layer's mash, where she had dropped it. Hugh O'Keeffe, the neighboring farmer, happened to find her because he was passing by, out for an early walk with his new hunting dog (a mean-looking German shorthaired pointer), and he had looked in to the chicken house to investigate the unusual racket Mary's chickens were making—he thought their alarm signaled an intruding fox or dog. Her chickens were all crowded at the other end of the house, perched on an abandoned settle Mary had told me the other day was originally from the kitchen of her cottage, before she made all sorts of Formica improvements a few years ago. It was her heart, people thought. She'd had a heart condition for a long while. Mary was seventy-nine—a good age.

Nora rapped on my door before daylight this morning to tell me the terrible news. She was so agitated, blurting out the details of the plans for the wake and funeral, and what Mary's nephew from Union Hall wanted her to do, that she stood there, twisting her hands over and over, almost violently, as she talked, until she looked down and exclaimed, "Oh, look at me, I'm the knitter without wool!" before she scurried off to her milking.

Mickey was still asleep, and I had been nervous as well as upset, standing in the open door clutching my bathrobe around my nakedness, concerned that he would call out to me or come downstairs while Nora was still there. I didn't know how Mickey would want his presence explained, or if his presence is supposed to be completely hidden.

I realized as the awfulness of Nora's words washed over my brain like ice water that I have no idea how long Mickey is going to stay. He and I hardly spoke once we went upstairs last night. The information we exchanged was not about schedules.

Nora asked me if I would be able to take a turn sitting with Mary's body through the night. She seems to have been put in charge of the preparations by the nephew. I had a hard time understanding her, because we were both so upset, but I gather there's something like a wake tonight, in Mary's cottage, and then tomorrow there will be a funeral and then a burial in the church-yard at the Protestant church in Clonakilty, beside George Carew, who's been sleeping alone in their double grave since 1944. My hands are trembling as I write. I cannot take this in.

I'm going to stop now and put this away, then make some breakfast for Mickey, and wake him up, if the smell of rashers and eggs doesn't. We have to talk.

I have a gnawing fear, a dread, that Mary's death is my fault. Am I losing my mind? What is happening? Surely I am in mourning for the death of an elderly woman with whom I was briefly acquainted. But why does it feel as though I'm in mourning for something in my life far more significant than that?

3rd of February, every kind of weather

I AM AN IDIOT. A naïve idiot.

So much has occurred in two days. This will be my last entry in the account book. I can only try to describe things as they happened.

The bacon and eggs were just ready when Mickey appeared at the bottom of the stairs, dressed in his clothes from the day before, startling me as I was getting milk from the tiny fridge under the counter. He's like a cat the way he can slip in and out of places. It must have been close to nine o'clock by then.

He grinned at the sight of—what, me, the food?—and came up behind me to catch me in an embrace as I stood with the milk carton in my hand. I poured him a cup of coffee from inside the circumference of his arms, and then we sat together while he wolfed down all of his breakfast and most of mine. I wasn't hungry. I almost burned the toast again, but Mickey looked up and sniffed and said he thought he smelled something burning, and I jumped up and caught it just in time—it didn't even need scraping. I felt like someone playing a part. Words came to mind and then just congealed in my chest. Why didn't he notice that something was wrong?

"Is there any jam?" he asked hopefully, swabbing up the last of the egg yolks on my plate from across the table with a nugget of toast.

Wordlessly, I went to the counter to get Mary's bramble jelly, which sat there in its little jar on the counter, not having heard the news. I placed it carefully on the table in front of him, and as I did so, a squeak of despair rose out of my chest and hit the back of my throat.

Mickey looked up and our eyes met. I didn't know him. I did not know this man sitting at my table, though his clotted semen was between my legs. He caught hold of my wrist, the burned hand with the bandage across the palm. I stood there, looking down at him. There was egg on the corner of his mouth. Whatever mix of dread and hope I had been feeling in these last few minutes seemed to coalesce into a terrible kind of icy despair.

"We had to, you know," he said so softly, so gently, so reasonably.

I knew this already, didn't I?

"Why?"

"Oh, Patricia, don't be naïve. Why? Because she would have told someone, that's why. Because she would have made a hames of our plans, no matter what her sympathies. Several lives would have been at risk, including your own."

I must have just stared. Mickey went on. "I *am* sorry, you know. I didn't think there would be call for wet work, especially once we'd got the picture safely here. I really do regret this. You must be more careful, Patricia."

I could feel my pulse roaring in my head. I felt deeply sick, hot, cold. A creeping nausea seemed to rise in my gut on the tide of those words. Mickey was someone I had invented for my own needs. Clearly, he had never really existed. Michael O'Driscoll from Rosscarbery was real enough, sitting here before me.

"How did you even know she saw the painting?" It seemed insane that we were having this conversation, that something this brutal could be discussed over breakfast. I sank back down into my chair because I could hardly stand up for another moment. I turned the chair away from the table so that I didn't have to look directly at Mickey. The way Mary had been unable to look at me only the morning before.

He waved a hand in the air, gesturing around the

room, indicating—what? I didn't understand, and then I did.

"The cottage is *bugged*? You *bugged* me?"

Mickey shrugged and buttered another piece of toast. "A routine security precaution," he said lightly. "Nothing personal. You're quite adorable altogether when you sing in the bath, by the way." He whistled a few halting bars of "King of the Road" and my humiliation was complete.

"I cannot believe this." God knows who was listening to us right now. I felt a creeping sensation up my back and arms: horripilation.

"Look, I'm sorry," Mickey said impatiently. "You've been a little bit had, and you'll lick your wounds and call me a load of shite on a stick, and that's fair enough. But mind you get over it fast, because we've got a larger matter on our hands at the moment."

"No. Wait." I could hear my voice outside my head, as if it belonged to someone else. "I need to know something from you right now."

He nodded, waiting for me to continue.

"Mickey. Who *are* you? What's real? What about... us? Last night? Has any of it mattered to you, or was it all part of the plan?" I hated my own pleading tone, the clichés. The thought that Mickey's confederates were listening right at this moment.

"Don't be simple, Patricia," he said. "No, wait—hear me out." I had started to get up from the table. "You're asking what's real. Let me answer you. The plan is real," he said slowly, choosing his words with evident care. "Retribution, righting the wrong, that's the only certain reality for me. I've grown very fond of you, and I wasn't plannin' on that a'tall, but it's happened. So that's real. We've had a great run together. It really wasn't something I was lookin' for, though I've been lonely enough, but then you came along—"

"How? How exactly did I come along?" I had never asked Mickey enough about this before, though he had told me at the outset that I had been selected as a candidate for approaching because my profile was such a good match, given my art expertise and my Irish sympathies. Why hadn't I questioned him more closely before I jumped in so blindly? I must have been crazy. I had confused destiny with feuding and violence.

"Your name came up."

"That's it? My name came up? Where? In some IRA bunker in downtown Derry? What exactly do you mean, my name came up?"

"Patricia, when are you going to learn the cardinal rules—you don't need to know that, so I'm not going to say. Let's just leave it that a Foley's regular spoke your name with much admiration and proposed Patricia Dolan as a fine candidate for the job. Which, by the way, you've been, right up to this moment here."

"Foley's? Foley's in the South End? Pete's Foley's?"

Mickey looked at me with a little condescending smile on his lips. He reached over and patted the back of my bandaged hand. "You see what a little knowledge does? Just makes trouble. Just makes you wonder about things you shouldn't wonder about." I snatched my hand away and he lunged across the table and grabbed my wrist and slammed my hand back down on the table. The searing pain was a great deal less than the sting of knowing that Mickey would deliberately hurt me this way. I fought back tears, hating my tears, hating Mickey.

"Now you listen," he hissed at me. "You were proposed for inclusion by an old fella who's done a bit of work here and there for us called Jimmy Leary. All right? Does knowing that little bit more improve anything a'tall?"

"Jimmy Leary? Pete's old friend from the squad? Jimmy Leary who taught me how to drive? Oh my God."

"Now can we leave it? We've got more urgent business, Patricia."

"No! We fucking well can't leave it! *You* listen! I want to know what happened to Mary! And I'm going to the police if that old lady was murdered because of me," I said, struggling to locate a clear place to land from this terrifying height. "Would you kill *me* if I said I was going to the police? No, gardai, isn't that it? The guards? I could walk down to the call box in front of Nolan's right now. What did you do? Have that fake telephone guy break her neck? While you were here keeping me busy? Is that what they train you to do in the IRA?" My hand was throbbing.

"Patricia." Mickey's voice was harsh. "Look at me." I did. There was a coldness in his eyes that I had not seen before this moment. It scared me.

"Now *you* listen. Listen well to what I'm saying to you. Pete Dolan." He enunciated carefully, as if reading the caption to a picture. His voice was steel, his words thin and cold, turned on a lathe of cruelty. "Pete Dolan, a true Irish patriot and sympathizer over the years. A retired detective in Boston, Massachusetts, in the US of A, a fella who lent a hand here and there without feelin' the need to ask one single question, because he was a patriot and that was enough.

"You might say that in his years of service to the police force, yer man has probably acquired numerous enemies garnered over many long years of service protecting the citizenry of Boston from crime. Now consider the crowd of small-time killers and thieves and thugs who were sent away for a time because of the diligent efforts of Pete Dolan. There must be dozens of them about. Those men have long memories and empty pockets, Patricia. Fellas like that, blamers and begrudgers, it doesn't take much to inspire. Let's not have another word on this subject now, all right?"

"You wouldn't."

"*You* wouldn't."

There was a very long silent moment in that kitchen, during which time pieces of my heart tore loose and shattered.

"Look, now. This isn't goin' our way, Patricia. Listen to me a minute here." Mickey's accent had begun to thicken up like porridge over the last few minutes. "It's not a doddle after all. They've refused our demand. Do you understand what I'm sayin' to ya?"

"Not exactly. Buckingham Palace won't give you the money?"

"*Buckingham* bloody *Palace* won't even acknowledge that they've got a picture gone *missin'*. They've *hung The Music Lesson* back on the *wall*." He punctuated his words with a heavy closed fist that made the crockery jump.

"That's not possible."

"Why not? You're the great art expert who came up with the plan to use a fake. Do you think you're the only one about with that sort of imagination? Apparently not."

"They're hanging our fake? It wasn't that good."

"I thought our fake looked real enough—I couldn't spot the difference. 'Twas real enough to do the trick. No, according to our man inside—a sleeper who's worked his way up from kitchen cleaner to footman over the last twelve years—it's a nineteenth-century copy, quite a reasonable one, apparently. They're ignoring us and topping us at our own game. Betty Windsor didn't seem to twig to it. They've hung it in a darkish corner in private quarters. They said it had been cleaned and that's why it might look a bit brighter." Mickey was very bitter, spitting out his words.

"So now what?" I was, frankly, disappointed, crazy as that sounds at this juncture. I still believed that what we were doing had made its own kind of sense, and I was also getting concerned about the disposition of *The Music Lesson* itself. It didn't seem likely that they would just let me keep it, take it home. Up until this moment, I had always envisioned it back on the wall in London where it belonged, having served its purpose, none the worse for wear.

"It's like the fuckin' Gardner all over again," Mickey muttered, tipping back in his chair and cleaning under his fingernails with the point of the bread knife.

Despite everything else I had heard up to that moment, I was really surprised.

"You were involved with the Gardner theft? It was the IRA that took those paintings in 1990? Those men dressed in police uniforms were IRA? Where are the paintings now? What happened?"

"Who here has been sayin' anything a'tall about the IRA, lassie?" Mickey said in a cruelly bantering tone. "What makes ya think the IRA knows anythin' about any of these doin's? The IRA is terribly busy occupyin' itself just now jumpin' through some little hoops held up by yer man Mr. Adams."

"The IRA," I said stupidly. "The Irish Republican Army. Come on, Mickey. Stop it. Stop talking like Lady Chatterley's lover. The IRA. Isn't that what this is all about? Isn't that what I'm working for, with you?"

"Well, you've got some of the letters right." He laughed. "Try IRLO—Irish Republican Liberation Organization. The lads to call when you want to get the job done. We're what the newspapers call a splinter group. No muckin' around just tryin' to get a wee little chair or two at Stormont."

"You're not IRA? You're IRLO?"

He saluted me with an exaggerated flourish.

"You were involved with the Gardner theft?" I couldn't get over it, couldn't make my mind know this.

"Not me personally," Mickey said. "But me lads were. Yer man Leary knows a thing or two about it, I'd say. Pete himself rounded up some extra uniforms and shields for Leary, though he was never told who needed them or for what purpose. But he must have read the news and added it up. Did yer old man never say a word to you about that?"

I tried to think, though my mind was skidding. Pete, actually involved with the IRA, or the IRLO, or whatever it was? This was really too much to comprehend. I was in free fall.

"No, no—I had no idea." I had a horrible thought. "Did you and Pete know each other before we went up at Christmas? Was that all a setup, as well?"

"Not really. You could say we knew *of* each other, like. He's a good man, yer da."

"So, what did happen with the Gardner?" I was in such confusion, I was trying to hold on to the most easily grasped detail of this horrendous flow of revelations. Betrayal is a body blow to the soul.

"It ended badly. You're not going to like the story, Patricia. Yer precious pictures are probably at the bottom of the sea."

"What happened?"

"Ah, you've become a connoisseur of big plans to steal art now, have ya? Well, there's no harm in telling you what I know in this instance, and you deserve a little treat. This is how the cards fell: Declan McGlinchey and his lads organized it from over here. It was the day after Saint Paddy's. I don't know all the bits and pieces, but there was a trawler all rigged out, fishing legal out of Gloucester, and a gang of our fellas were crew—some of them used to work the big trawlers out of Union Hall, and they said the fishing in those American waters wasn't half-bad, though it was perishin' cold half the year—and they had the job done and they were well out to sea when they ran into some kind of bad trouble and started taking in water, and they didn't radio for help until it was too late because they had all those pictures down in the hold and they knew they'd be pinched if they were boarded. They never even had a chance to make the ransom demand. Who knows what kind of trouble they were after havin'. They disappeared—probably went straight down."

"What do you think happened?" I was considering *The Concert* on the bottom of the sea. Is there any light at all, or is it completely dark under all that ocean? It was odd to chat this way with Mickey, as if we were still us. As if we were discussing a movie one of us had seen a long time ago.

"McGlinchey thought one of the lads might have had a plan of his own, and there was some sort of altercation or sabotage."

"Then how do you know the renegade didn't kill the others, sink the boat, and get away in a dinghy with the paintings?"

"Oh, Patricia, you've got a fine enterprisin' criminal mind, you really do," Mickey said admiringly. "There's some who think that's what happened, all right. It's possible, of course, that the paintings weren't on the trawler in the first place, or that it went exactly that way, with a plan and a dinghy and someone with a load of patience. I know a lad who swears he knows the fella who knows the fella who has the whole bloody art collection in some warehouse outside Boston. But don't you think we'd have had a word from him by now?"

"Maybe Declan heard from him and didn't tell you," I shot back. "Maybe you're the one who's been left out."

"That would be neat," Mickey said, tipping his chair back down to hit the floor. "Decky McGlinchey was buried just six months after the Gardner went down. Shot dead, by occupyin' forces, of course."

"Oh, of course," I answered, matching his tone. Being angry helped keep me from my fear, my despair.

"So here's our plan," Mickey said, eyeing me carefully.

"'Our' plan, Mickey?"

"Look, I know this is rough for you," he said, slightly apologetic now. "But we're not done here. Listen, now. We want to go public with the theft. Get word out to television stations and newspapers. Expose the lyin' cunts at Buckingham Palace. If we can't get our money, we'll get good value anyway—let the world know we're a force to be reckoned with. It won't have been a wasted effort, you see. We'll make the best of it."

"You don't need my advice to help you send out a press release."

"Christ, no, Patricia, don't you get it? We're going to make a home movie. We're going to videotape the destruction of *The Music Lesson* and send copies of the tape around the world. It'll be great altogether. Our public-relations machine versus theirs. People don't like bein' kept in the dark. Talk about a lesson. They can listen to our music, dance to our piper."

◻

I really hated him then. I really did. I hated him already for what had happened to Mary, for who and what he seemed to be, for who and what he turned out not to be, but this was a turning point. I knew the Troubles were an evil situation, but now I was looking at evil incarnate.

"So here's what we need from you," he went on, unbelievably. He had no idea who I was, none whatsoever. We were a pair, Mickey and I. He had invented me to suit himself. "We were thinking to burn it, but one of the lads thought it wouldn't go very easily, and might just smolder and smoke, go off a damp squib. Not the best thing for the six o'clock news. What do you think? You know about the paint and all, how it would burn, maybe. Maybe we should douse it with petrol first. You know, for the dramatic effect, like?"

I thought for a few minutes. I thought about a great many things, all of my options. Mickey has always been very good with silences. He waited patiently. I had an answer then.

"Murder it," I said.

"What do you mean?" he asked suspiciously.

"Kill it. Look, you've got an automatic weapon around someplace, probably, right? Or can't you tell me that?" Mickey nodded a noncommittal yes, slowly, considering. "So put the painting against a wall, with a newspaper of the day to show the date, and then have someone blast it to bits with a few rounds. Isn't that your style, anyway? Execution? It'll look good on camera. Violent. It'll just turn into nothing, into sawdust, in front of the world."

Mickey looked at me with an appreciative smile.

"Patricia, you're fantastic. Once again, grace under pressure. You've really come through for me. Don't think I'm not grateful."

I knew what I needed to do. *The Music Lesson* had taught me. Vermeer's is an art that chooses among things, rectifying them. It's a kind of genius that comes from never judging beforehand. One must ask what is called for, what one's subject wants. One must let oneself be surprised.

I went to the wake at Mary's cottage that evening. Nora had told me to come at about eleven. It was cold, but clear, and dark, with only the faintest illumination from a new moon.

I can hardly say what I had done with the rest of that horrible day. Mickey had several conversations on a cell phone. We barely spoke. Mickey was distracted, keyed up. I took a nap, and when I woke at one point, I could hear more than one male voice downstairs, so I didn't dare go down, and then I went back to sleep for a while, and then it was evening. When I did go downstairs, it was when Mickey was taking a bath and the cottage was otherwise empty. The settle was open—someone had slept on that old mattress. I put several dirty teacups into the sink. There were cigarette butts in one of them, floating in an inch of milky tea. Mickey—or someone—had heated up some tomato soup from a can. It smelled like vomit to me. I sat down to wait until it was time to leave. I tried unsuccessfully to finish *The Book of Evidence*. I kept thinking about *The Music Lesson*.

There is a consciousness in that painting that amounts to integrity made visible. Ultimately, to regard this magnificent creation of Vermeer's is to see the world being thought. In her contemplative isolation, the woman looks up from her music and regards us, and she asks us to take a position, she commands us to exist, to see ourselves.

Mickey seemed to be staying in the cottage. He said he figured that I wouldn't be back until morning, if I was going to be part of Mary's wake retinue. I was glad that there would be no question about who would sleep where. I felt as though I were moving underwater. As I went to the door, bundled against the dark, cold walk up to Mary's, Mickey followed me and took me by the arm.

"How's the hand?" he asked in a low voice.

"Fine," I said shortly, not looking at him. It hurt like hell, actually.

"Sorry."

"Uh-huh." I kept willing Mickey to stay away from me in the small spaces of the cottage. I couldn't stand his few light, perhaps accidental touches. *Hard, isolate, stoic, and a killer* floated to mind. These were the words D. H. Lawrence used for James Fenimore Cooper's Leatherstocking.

"Your best bet is a departure in the morning, after the funeral, of course," he said. "You've got the Aer Lingus ticket, and you can do what you like, but you might want to consider your options—there are freighters bound for America in and out of Cobh every week, and the passenger accommodations can be nice enough. The grub's not bad, and it's a decent way to pass a fortnight. It might suit you, a slow return, some time off on yer own, like. Most of the Panamanian ships don't ask a lot of questions. I can give you some names if you want."

"Questions don't bother me. I don't have anything to hide," I said.

"No, so you don't." He sighed. "I'll write down the information—it'll be on the table for you. So that's it, then. You can have a last look in the morning at yer little picture, I promise you that." He leaned down as if to kiss me, and I froze. He stopped for a moment and then I felt his lips brush my forehead for an instant. "Ah, Patricia," he whispered. "If I had a life that let me love anyone a'tall, I would love you. Please believe me that I wasn't playing games with you. You have to understand what it's like here. Perpetual humiliation. We're all trapped in it. We *have* to struggle. We *have* to resist. It's a maiming thing, this great fuckin' hatred."

I had brought just one skirt, rather dowdy, dark blue corduroy, and I was wearing it, though I would have to wear it again to the funeral service in the morning.

As I approached the door to Mary's cottage, it opened and Kieran O'Mahoney came out. Several cats emerged as well and streaked into the darkness. Who would feed them? I realized I hadn't seen Tiggy in a few days. Oh, well, Irish cats seem to know how to earn a living. Kieran didn't see me. He stopped and crossed himself, then stopped again to light a cigarette. He went to his car, which was wedged into a gap in the wall that runs along the road.

I waited in the shadows beside Mary's chicken house, in no mood for a conversation, while he took a long, hissing piss against the wall, got into his car, reversed it into Mary's yard, and pulled out into the lane to drive away.

With two other women from the parish, Nora had washed Mary's body and laid it out in a white garment on the bed. I realized it must be a shroud. I had never seen one. Mary looked tiny, as if death had shrunk her down, sucked out something that had taken up space inside her.

I didn't know what the protocols were, but following some instinct, I went to the bed, knelt down, and found comfort in the ancient familiarity of a Hail Mary and an Our Father.

Nora introduced me to Mary's nephew, Peter Carew, and his wife, Kathleen, who is enormously pregnant. Peter is a tall, diffident-seeming man in his twenties, with a limp handshake. He'll inherit Mary's cottage. Kathleen took me by the sleeve and began to explain, rather defensively, that the minister from Clonakilty had called in earlier, briefly, and had authorized them to carry on.

Kathleen, like all of Mary's neighbors, is Catholic, and they were doing things in the traditional way they knew, despite the burial being out of a Protestant church in the morning. Peter, she confided to me, "is a Godless heathen with no religion at all."

There were candles guttering on several surfaces. White sheets were draped about on some of the furniture. Where had I seen this room before? Hogarth? Brueghel? Jan Steen?

The bedroom was narrow and stuffy, so after standing awkwardly for a few minutes, exchanging small talk with the Carews and Nora and two other women who were sitting on three chairs in a straight row, like children playing at being on a train, I went back down.

There were several other people in the house, some

of whom I knew from the village, but others were complete strangers to me. Food and drinks were laid out on the table in the parlor. It felt like Mary's hospitality, somehow, and I wanted to eat something, having barely eaten all day, feeling comforted being in Mary's house, which felt familiar, though I had never been inside before.

I ate a rather mayonnaisey ham sandwich, standing by the table, looking around at Mary's things—doilies, seashells, Staffordshire figurines, some terrible nineteenth-century ancestral portraits in gilt plaster frames. An old man I recognized as one of the pub regulars who stare at me when I go into the village, whose Sunday best suit radiated rich camphor vapors, leaned against me and reached across the table to pour himself another drink of whiskey, finishing the bottle. He held it up to the light and squinted at it, as though he thought he might discover something in the empty bottle.

"Miss, do ya know why they call an empty whiskey bottle a dead soldier, miss?" he asked me politely.

"No."

"Because, miss, the spirit is departed. Ya see? The bottle is empty and the spirit is departed. A dead soldier. That's what they call it. They do. Did ya know that, now, did ya, miss?" He put the bottle down on its side and rubbed his hands together, delighted with himself.

"Donal, stop yer flirtin' with the American lady,"

warned an almost identically dressed man who was sitting by the television set. The picture was on, but the sound was turned down. Its flickering blue light spilled across his lap. *Dynasty* was on.

"Donal's like a dog with two tails when he has a chance to speak to a pretty gel. Have a bit of cake, dearie?" asked Hugh O'Keeffe's wife. Wanting to be polite, feeling very much the stranger in their midst, I took the piece she held out, though evidently no one else had been in the mood for cake. It was heavily stuccoed with pink frosting that tasted of lard.

"It's very good," I said after one small bite.

Hugh O'Keeffe looked up from where he was sitting at the table. I realized he was drunk. I realized that most of the men in the room were drunk. "'Tis Orla's speciality," he said, drawing out the word to five syllables. "Donkey's gudge."

"I never," Orla O'Keeffe assured me, resting her enormous work-roughened hand on my arm.

The Carews came downstairs and I sensed currents in the air that I did not understand. They weren't liked.

The door opened and Annie Dunne stood there, the bad fairy at the christening. She was dressed in an old-fashioned black skirt that looked vaguely Spanish. She eyed everyone in the room suspiciously. Some cats bolted through the door as it closed, fanning a welcome gust of cold air into the stale parlor.

"'Tis a shame, oh, 'tis a shame," Annie scolded generally. "And you"—she fixed me in her sights—"you, miss, you were the last to see Mary alive, you know. 'Tis a fact. The guards told me. They interviewed me, of course, asked me questions, like. They knew who would know what's what in Ballyroe, they did."

"They did no such thing; they stopped in to buy some fags and crisps is all," Donal muttered. "'Twas Annie did the interviewin'."

People trickled in and out for the next couple of hours, but by 2:00 A.M., only Nora, Orla O'Keeffe, and I were left. The Carews left early, a little embarrassed, I think, to be ducking the responsibility of the wake night, though Nora shooed them out, insisting that Kathleen needed to get off her feet. Nora and I washed the dishes—the "ware"—without much conversation. She told me that she had known Peter since he was a boy, when he used to visit Mary for a fortnight every August.

"He never was much of a lad, so it was a bit of a shock, all right, when he had to marry that Kathleen O'Leary so quickly. Her father was none too pleased. He had bigger ambitions for his youngest daughter than seeing her married off to a Brit with weak tea in his veins, though Peter did the right thing by her, I'll give him that," Nora said.

"This just happened?" I was momentarily confused.

"Oh, mercy no, the one under the apron's her sixth. It's become a habit with them."

Drying Mary's cups and plates with her dishcloth made me sad, made me miss her. I wondered what Peter would do with the cottage. Sell it? Rent it out? Nora left then, saying she needed to nip down the road for an hour to check on an infected cow her boys were minding for her.

I went up to Orla with a fresh cup of tea for her. There seemed to be a traditional requirement to mind Mary's body at every moment—I realized that she had never been left unattended all through the evening.

I was glad when Orla said she needed to put her legs up, if I didn't mind (she's got some kind of circulation disorder, from the looks of her swollen ankles), and got to her feet heavily. She went down the stairs slowly, one at a time. I could hear her teacup rattling on its saucer as she progressed.

I was alone with Mary then for a while. Long enough to tell her the things I needed to tell her.

Who was she to me? I didn't know her very well. She was an elderly Scottish lady who enjoyed reading a bit, loved her cats and her garden. We will always be bound together. She'll keep the secret well.

At some point, Nora came back and Orla went home. Nora and I sat in silence beside the bed, nodding in and out of sleep, the candles burning down to the saucers. I dreamed of an endless sea that turned to green fields. I started to cross the fields, but then the land under my feet turned to water again, the hills merely frozen waves now beginning to churn once more. I woke, thinking, *calenture*. Twice through the rest of the night Nora began to recite the Rosary and I joined her both times. I fell more deeply asleep in my chair after that, and when I woke again, it was daylight. My neck hurt the way it does when you've slept on a train. The undertaker was rapping on the door impatiently. The hearse was in the yard, an enormous vintage hearse with glass sides.

Kevin Donohue and his assistant pulled the coffin out onto a wheeled dolly of some kind and opened the lid. They were in narrow dark suits, and they looked like extras from a movie. The coffin was empty. Of course it would be, but the emptiness was somehow a strange sight. The tufted red satin lining was cheap-looking in the harsh morning light. Nora was rattling things in the kitchen, preparing yet another pot of tea. The Irish hold a deep belief that enough cups of tea are the antidote to anything. Donohue came in with his assistant and the four of us sat in awkward silence and had tea and some stale biscuits from a tin box that tasted as if they were left over from Christmas.

Nora and I helped them wrap Mary in a white sheet, and then they wound another coarser white cloth around her until she was completely wrapped, like a tiny mummy. Between the two of them they carried Mary's body on a canvas stretcher down the narrow stairs. They had to tilt her almost upright to clear the bottom step.

They placed her in the coffin and fastened down the lid. Although Nora had explained to me that Mary would be put into her coffin as she was, in her shroud, and there would be no dressing of the corpse because the coffin would be closed, Nora looked troubled at this moment and muttered to me, "A closed-coffin funeral. That's how they do it for the Church of Ireland crowd. It isn't right. It's not our way. Not a'tall. Not a proper removal a'tall."

Donohue heard her and said, "Sorry, Nora, orders from himself above in Clon. It's the way that crowd likes to do it." Not that it matters, but I really disliked the man. The Uriah Heep of Clonakilty. The coffin slid into its slot and the doors were closed. Donohue got behind the wheel, his assistant beside him, both of them wearing silly plastic sunglasses, and the hearse glided off, looking horribly wrong on this familiar little stretch of road. I watched it until it was out of sight around a bend in the lane, and then I set off down the road to pack up my things and change for the funeral.

Nora called after me that I could sit in with her family if I liked, and I didn't know what she meant until she explained that they would give me a ride in their car to the church in Clonakilty in an hour's time, once she had got the milking done. I accepted gratefully, not having thought how I would get there.

The cottage seemed empty in a different way than it ever had before. Mickey was nowhere in evidence as I packed my bag. He had left me information about the freighters in Cobh, and a bus schedule. Very thoughtful. I put on my nicest sweater and hoped I looked respectable enough. My hair was limp—I hadn't washed it in five days. I caught a glimpse of myself in a window reflection as I set my bag by the door. I looked terrible, pale and haggard. Why not? I left some jeans on the top to change into, and otherwise everything I wanted to take home was in that bag except for this notebook, which I thought to keep with me in my handbag, in the event that someone might go through my things.

The ride to Clonakilty and back was nauseating, owing to Pat O'Driscoll's terrible driving, the winding roads, a bad muffler, and the mixture of camphor and body odor that wafted off the entire O'Driscoll clan. I was jammed in the backseat between two of the sons, the other two having stayed home to mind the cows. The funeral itself was unremarkable and perfunctory, attended mostly by the local congregation—few of the neighbors from Ballyroe had made the drive. The minister seemed cold to me, the service rote. It had nothing to do with the Mary Carew I had known that little bit.

She had a headstone, with her name engraved on it

already, and her birth date, too, followed by a dash. It would be but the work of a moment for the stonecutter to add the year of her death. The service was done, the minister gone back inside the church, most everyone dispersed, and I stayed on, watching the coffin go into the ground. I had said my good-bye to Mary when I was alone with her in the night. Now I closed my eyes for a moment, listening to the sounds of the spades digging into the mound of soil and then hearing the clods of earth hit the polished wood.

Katie's funeral was a graveside service. Our friends had gathered under the trees in the cemetery on that terrible day, and what I remember most clearly about it is the sound of the clods of earth hitting the wooden lid of her little casket, knowing she was inside it, cold and alone. They tell me I grabbed a spade and shoveled frantically, as if to fill the hole by myself, until Sam took the spade from my hands and then our friends took turns filling the grave with dirt while Sam held me. What sour despair. We were two wretched people, each of us alone in our grief. We just never could fit back together.

For a moment I pictured Mary. I tried to imagine the interior of her coffin, the utter darkness, where no light would ever penetrate again. I didn't walk away until I had seen the grave diggers shovel enough dirt back into the hole to cover the coffin completely. Everyone had left. Nora's family was waiting in the car, staring at me through fogged windows. "'Tis not our custom to watch the actual burial," Nora said reprovingly as I got in.

I walked down to Gortbreac Cove from the O'Driscolls' farm. There was a muddy car parked in front of the cottage, the kind Nora calls an old banger, with hideous, filthy-looking tiger-striped seat covers and one of the back windows filled in with corrugated plastic and duct tape. I went in, and Mickey was sitting at the table with two other men, drinking tea and eating Hob Nob biscuits. ("One nibble and you're nobbled.") One of them was the Telecom Eireann man, and the other one was Willy Hayes, the postman. What's one more disappointment?

The painting was on the table.

The three men each raised a finger in laconic greeting, a characteristic Cork salute, the way they wave at one another when they meet on the road on their tractors or in their cars. I will miss this place. Ignoring the Telecom guy, I looked questioningly at Willy for a moment, and he nodded with a small shrug of acknowledgment.

"Change of plan," Mickey said. What now? I was suddenly frightened. I really thought for that moment that they had decided to kill me. "Back to plan A. We can't risk the noise factor. Though your suggestion was a good one. So we've got the petrol organized with some old hay from the shed."

"You're going to burn it?"

"Yes, that's what I'm saying. We've been waiting for you. Did they do the old girl up nicely?"

I didn't answer him. I took the painting off the table and walked across the room to see it in the light by the window.

"I'm taking the glass off—you don't want glass for this," I said.

I followed them, carrying the painting. We went in a silent procession out to the side yard, where I had seen indications of past bonfires. It was very still. Most everybody in Gortbreac was probably sitting down to their dinner, their midday meal.

A moldy bale of hay and a red plastic gasoline container stood beside one of the ash heaps. The Telecom guy took out a palm-sized camcorder from the pocket of his jacket and unscrewed the lens cap.

"For feck's sake," he instructed, "nobody speak—we want no voices on this tape. Nothin' to distinguish location—I'm keepin' a tight focus."

Mickey spread the hay tenderly into a comfortable-looking loose nest and then Willy laid a copy of the day's *Irish Times* with the headline showing on top of the hay. There had been a slurry spill in Mallow and the fish kill in the Blackwater was going to hurt the angling season.

I laid the painting down on the newspaper, gently,

as if I were putting a sleeping baby into a crib. The colors all looked muddy to me, worn thin, muted by a strange chiaroscuro sky of shifting clouds. Her eyes were empty. Her hands were flat and meaningless; there was no form, no grace. There was no magic in this painting. A dull afternoon wind seemed to rinse the air of clarity.

Mickey sluiced the petrol over everything. Willy struck a match. It was so quiet, I could hear the video camera humming. He threw the match down and a sheet of flame shot up at once, with ugly black smoke furling at its edge.

It was a very small painting, and it was gone in another moment. The blackened wood panel continued to burn for another few minutes. The Telecom man zoomed in close, kneeling down, to show the charred wafery pieces of frame that still boxed a rectangular form. I started to walk away. Mickey was shoveling the black remnants into a heap with a stick, then he splashed the rest of the petrol onto the remaining wisps of hay. I turned back for one last look at Mickey. His face was a blank. A spark ignited and flames leapt up. Whatever was left of the panel was soon pale ash, snowing upward on the breeze.

I had nothing more to say to Mickey. I have nothing to say to anyone right now. I can't imagine that changing for a long time. I am empty. I have seen the last of *The Music Lesson*. I changed my clothes and was out the door with my bag. I did not look back again.

I was only halfway to Ballyroe when I heard a tractor behind me, and as I stood aside to let it pass, I heard it slow and stop. I turned, and it was Billy Houlihan. I will never know if he was heading into the village anyway or if he saw me with my bag and followed me. Maybe it was just one of life's chance symmetries. He gave me a ride into the village, where I could catch the bus to Clonakilty, where I would catch the bus to Cobh.

"Leavin' us, are ya?" he shouted above the roar of his tractor as I climbed onto the back. I only nodded. When he left me off in Ballyroe a few minutes later, he gave me a hand down and I felt his rough calloused grip give me an extra squeeze. I held on tight for a moment, and then I let go. He was the only person to whom I said good-bye.

I am writing these final pages in a little bed and breakfast in Cobh. I've been up all night, and in a short while I'll go in to my last Irish breakfast. I'm starved. I'm booked on a Panamanian freighter that sails this afternoon with mixed cargo—timber, coal, machine parts— bound for Halifax, which, given the patterns of history, seems just right. It was a good idea of Mickey's. Flying back to my old life in a matter of hours would have been an impossibly abrupt transition. I need this time. I've sent a postcard to Pete telling him where I am and the approximate day we're likely to make landfall.

I will return to New York, back to a life where nothing will have changed and everything will have changed, a life in which nothing will be the same and everything will be the same. What I miss most about Mickey is possibility, what might have been. I will miss the way I was with him, the way I thought about the future. I will miss this land of eloquent storytellers who cannot distinguish truth from fiction.

Soon enough, I will return to my job at the Frick Art Reference Library. I have already figured out precisely where this little notebook will be safe for a very long time. Surely, reader, I don't have to describe exactly which volume of bound duplicate publications concerning art forgeries I have chosen as the ideal resting place for this account, because if you are reading my words, you know where you found them. When you've finished reading, I can only hope that you will see the necessity of returning this account to its hiding place. Please have the grace and courage to put it back.

I hope I live long enough to make my peace with a world full of people who look but do not see, who listen but do not hear.

I will sail from this land, as Michael Dolan sailed, heading for the New World, hoping to make a better life. In truth, my days here will lead me to make a better life than the one I had before. My hand will heal. I hope I have a scar.

I will have one very brief conversation with Pete about Mickey, in which we will agree that we'll never discuss it again, and then we won't discuss it again. I hope Pete has a good few years left, and I hope he has an easy death.

I will probably become quite eccentric in my old age. I plan to have a lot of cats. Although I expect to live out my years alone, I am never alone. Some of the people I love the most aren't alive in the world, but they are alive in me. I think of my mother, and the ways I might be like her. I can begin to think of Katie, and the ways she might have been like me. Even if life has to be a series of losses, then I still choose life.

I brought along my own *Music Lesson* reproduction, of course. One of the deluxe ones, purchased from the Frick gift shop with my employee discount. I kept it under the stair, with this notebook. I thought it might come in handy. It fit into the frame perfectly. It burned quite nicely, too. I was frightened for a moment there, when Willy struck the match and I realized that it could have an acrylic ground that would flare up in a telltale way, or the panel might peel into plywood layers, or something awful like that. It would have cost me my life, I'm sure. But it burned true.

And I think of Mary Carew. She would have enjoyed, I believe, having *The Music Lesson* next to her heart for all eternity. Because that's where it is, in the graveyard in Clonakilty, in County Cork, in the Republic of Ireland, in the world, in the universe.